The Wolf Pack Bloodlines BOX SET
Complete Series

Amelia Wilson

CONTENTS

Lone Wolf to Alpha

Origins of the Alpha

The Fate of the Alpha

Copyright © 2020 by Amelia Wilson
All rights reserved.

In no way is it legal to reproduce, duplicate, or transmit any part of this document in either electronic means or in printed format. Recording of this publication is strictly prohibited, and any storage of this document is not allowed unless with written permission from the publisher. All rights reserved.

This book is a work of fiction. Names, characters, places and incidents are either the product of the author's imagination or are used fictitiously, and any resemblance to actual persons, living or dead, events or locales is entirely coincidental.

Lone Wolf to Alpha
The Wolf Pack Bloodlines Series

Amelia Wilson

Table of Contents:

Prologue

Chapter 1

Chapter 2

Chapter 3

Chapter 4

Chapter 5

Chapter 6

Chapter 7

Chapter 8

Chapter 9

Chapter 10

Chapter 11

Chapter 12

Chapter 13

Epilogue

Prologue

"Thomas?"

"Angie. Are you okay?" Thomas shifted his head as much as he could to stare into his wife's eyes. Glass from the broken windshield littered the inside of the flipped car. Despite the pain, Thomas reached for his wife. His fingertips barely grazed her face before dropping down again.

Chilly air blasted through the open windshield, smacking Angie on the face as she peered through into the darkness. On the horizon, she saw a shadow moving through the trees, racing closer to her. Although she wanted to scream, her voice was silent. Every nerve in her body tingled as she allowed the heat from her core to rise up and shroud her.

With all the strength she could muster, Angie tore the seat belt that kept her strapped into the car. Her body slumped to the ground. Her ribs cracked, as she hit the twisted metal of what was once was the roof. The hard crunching sound of boots stomping in the snow filled her ears as she struggled to unpin her leg, which was wedged between the dashboard and the seat.

"She's not here," Angie cried out to the darkness.

"Where is she?" A rough deep voice asked as Angie tried to keep her eyes on the shadow as it shifted and darted between the trees.

"You will never find her."

"That is where you are mistaken. Even if she isn't here now, she will return. This place will call to her and she will have no choice but to find her way back."

The shadow grew closer, coming up on Angie until she felt his hot breath on her neck. "One more chance."

"No." Angie hissed as the darkness consumed her.

Chapter 1

Kayla Dale stood beside her truck with her face buried in her jacket, as the frosty air nipped at her nose. Gentle white flakes drifted from the sky, cleansing the area with a white blanket of snow. Every so often the wind shifted filling her nostrils with the overpowering aroma of gas as she filled her truck up. Everything from the small neon sign to the trash cans overflowing with garbage repulsed her.

All she wanted to do was to hurry up and get back on the road.

When the nozzle clicked and the flow of gas stopped, she pulled the line back and replaced the hose. A swift flick of her wrist secured the gas cap and soon she could be on her way. She made her way through the snowy parking lot to the convenient store, with long strides. As she walked into the even dirtier store, the heat from the doors knocked her back.

In the corner of the store, three men sat on bar stools that lined the windows. From what Kayla could gather, they were the truckers who had pulled in to wait out the storm. Kayla shook her head as she searched the aisles for the snacks she would need to continue.

"I wouldn't drive through those woods at night, even if it was a clear night." Kayla overheard one man say in a raspy, hushed voice. She turned her head and a smile played at the corner of her lips. A heavy-set man with a long-sleeved shirt and thick beard was sipping causally from a cup. Kayla couldn't help but watch the steam rising from the top, swirling around the man's nose before vanishing into his beard. Next to him was a short man with dark hair and sober eyes that seemed to be withered from time and experience. Both kept their eyes locked on the road that led up to the mountain.

"I heard that highway is haunted," the man continued matter-of-factly. Kayla shook her head and turned back to the snacks hanging from the rack.

"It seems every year there are at least thirty people that die on that mountain pass." The second man stated. "When the bodies are found they say they look like they were attacked by wild animals."

"Demons more likely." The husky man chimed in as Kayla made her choice from the hanging racks and walked to the counter.

"Hello there, will this be all for you?" The lanky thin man behind the counter looked up from his paper as Kayla dropped her items down and reached for the wallet in her back pocket.

"Yep." Kayla turned her head towards the two men by the window. "Plus gas. Pump one please."

"Sure thing," the store clerk said as he rang her purchases up. Then he glanced at her with a strange look in his eyes. Kayla turned her attention back to the lanky man and waited for her total.

"You gonna be traveling in this, Miss?" The thin man behind the counter glanced out the large windows as Kayla slapped money down onto the counter.

"I've driven in worse."

"Yeah, but the television is saying this is going to be the worst storm we've had in a decade. You sure you want to be headed out in it? Don't you think you should stay in here where it's nice and warm?" The thin man had greasy hair and he leaned forward as he spoke. Kayla stepped back, revolted by the look in his eyes.

"I can handle myself."

"Suit yourself. That will be $32.97." The man pulled the bills towards him and counted them slowly. Kayla stared out the window counting the seconds until she was free to move on.

"Looks like your all squared away. Drive safe out there. The roads can be slick."

"Sure." Kayla said as she collected her change and the small bag of goodies.

"Miss?" The husky voice called to her. Kayla paused with her hand on the door ready to push it open.

"You be careful. Strange things happen up on that mountain. You be sure to get over the top before night fall ya hear?"

Concern flashed across the man's face. For a moment Kayla wondered if he had daughters. She forced herself to smile and nodded once, before pushing through the glass barrier separating her from the cold. The frosty air slapped her face and without flinching she made a beeline for her truck. She had always enjoyed the snow. It was like water to her. Everything bad was washed away or hidden under the white blanket.

She pulled open her truck door and got in. With a quick twist of the key, the engine roared to life and she was gone. Only the road and the open spaces could tame her wild nature. It didn't matter if she was in rain, sleet, or blazing sunlight – anywhere outside was far better than a stuffy closed room.

Kayla flicked the radio on before turning up the heater. The rumble of the speakers drowned out everything else. All that was before her was the open road and she had no place in particular to go. With a smile etched across her face, she wove around the turns until tall thick woods blocked out the dreary light of day. It didn't take long before the snow began coming down in thicker clumps around her. The road was still visible, and she weaved along the road through the trees effortlessly.

"Where the hell is this coming from?" Kayla stared out the windshield as the snow drifted down from the sky in a white sheet that eventually began to block out the black asphalt. She kept her eyes locked on what little black she could see, as she turned the radio up and laughed. The memory of the two men at the gas station chatting like old wives tickled her.

"Superstitious old men." Kayla said she reached for her food.

Nothing was going to stop her from getting to the west coast. Not even a snow storm as severe as this one. She was from Maine and she had driven in plenty of blizzards before, but doubt began to bite into her nerves through the white. Maybe she should pull over and let it pass.

"Don't be stupid," she told herself and she hit the gas pedal, thrusting the truck faster down the unmarked road. "Just a little further and it will let up."

A little further had begun to be her mantra, and she knew it. Each passing mile only caused more snow to fall from the sky. What were once soft flakes were now huge balls that pelted her truck before breaking apart into smaller fragments. There were only two options, pull over or keep going. Despite her better judgment, the thrill turned her on and she pushed her little truck onward.

Kayla twisted the wheel trying to follow the tracks left behind by other vehicles, but the higher up the mountain she climbed, the harder the tracks were to follow. The snow drifted through the trees as the sun peaked through the clouds giving just enough light to see the next bend. She knew that she would need to get out of this forest before sunset or risk crashing.

"One more hour, and if it doesn't let up, I'll pull over."

She glanced at herself in the rearview mirror. Grey eyes, full and earnest stared back at her giving away her fear. There was no way she was going to allow herself to get stuck in that place after dark. It wasn't the stories she heard about these mountains that spooked her. She just didn't like the idea of sleeping in her truck. It was too cramped to get any real sleep.

But still, the stories of monsters living on this mountain did intrigue her. Maybe one night wouldn't hurt. After all, it's not every day you come face-to-face with myths and legends. But was it worth dying to be able to scratch that itch?

Chapter 2

The sun faded through the trees, casting long shadows over the white road. At each bend and twist Kayla found herself gasping, as her hopes to find something unusual rose and fell.

"There is nothing out here," she grumbled as she reached into her bag of goodies to pull out the last chip. As the flavor filled her mouth, she glanced over to the passenger's seat, searching for a drink to wet her whistle. When her eyes returned to the road she suddenly saw a black, furry creature in the middle of the road.

"Oh, shit." Kayla screamed as she jerked the wheel to the right, throwing her truck into the shoulder. She bounced and jerked about as the wheels barreled over fallen branches and rocks. Kayla slammed on her brakes trying to force her truck to come to a stop. The tires slipped over a patch of ice sending her truck careening into a large tree trunk. The screaming and wailing of twisted metal filled her ears and she braced herself for the final impact.

Kayla squeezed her eyes tight, waiting for her life to end. When it didn't, she peaked through her tightly closed eyelids. One by one, she peeled her fingers from the steering wheel and sucked in deep breaths.

"Are you crazy lady?" A deep voice beside her caused her to jump. The only thing keeping her from hitting her head on the roof of her car was the seat belt still strapped around her body. Kayla twisted her head to the open window. The frosty air nipped at her heated face, and she saw two white eyes staring at her in the darkness. She gasped and flinched as long arms reached in through the open space and touched her.

"Are you okay?" The man asked again. All Kayla could do was nod. Her voice left her as she froze in place staring at the hairy creature before her. As the snow drifted around them, the man nodded before pulling back the thick furry hood of his jacket revealing his true self.

"I am going to help you get out of this, but you are going to need to stay still, got it?" Kayla's eyes widened. Standing before her was a tall, handsome man with dark skin and high cheek bones. His long black hair swirled about his face with the breeze. Kayla couldn't help but keep her eyes locked on him as he worked to free her from the twisted metal and restrictive seat belt.

"What are you doing up here in this?" The man scolded as he worked. "Or did you not notice the blizzard?"

"I can drive in snow." Kayla fired back as she watched him pull out a long silver object from his side. With a flick of his wrist the seat belt no longer cut into her side.

"Apparently not."

"If it wasn't for you, standing in the middle of the road, I wouldn't have gotten into this mess." Kayla grumbled as the man ripped open the door. Her eyes widened as her door slammed into a nearby tree with a crash.

"Nate!"

Over the howling wind, Kayla's ears perked up at the sound of another voice. She stared at the man who clearly heard it too. He pressed his lips together tightly and let out two short whistle blasts before turning his attention back to Kayla.

"Come on," He said. You're going to have to come with us."

"Us? I don't think so. I don't know you. As far as I can see, you ran me off the road and now you want to kill me."

"Lady," The man, who was obviously Nate, pressed his eyebrows together into a tight line as his jaw clamped down. "If I wanted to kill you, you would be dead already. But hey, if that is what you want." Nate stepped back and turned around and started to walk back into the snowy fields. Kayla paused for a moment before climbing out of the truck.

Her legs were stiff and so was her neck. She knew there was no way she could survive the mountain without shelter and she debated following Nate into the woods.

"What have we here?" An unfamiliar voice spoke inches from Kayla's ears. She spun around. Her heart pumping as she raised her fists up into tight balls ready to strike. Laughter broke out from the darkness as Kayla tried to place where it was coming from.

"Jessie, enough."

"Oh come on."

"No. Now let's go. And grab her too while you are at it."

Before Kayla could protest, she was up in the air, flung over a furry coat. Although she couldn't complain about the cold anymore, now that she was snuggled into the warmth of her assailant's furry jacket, she did manage to kick and flail in protest at being picked up.

"Will you stop squirming," the man grumbled as his arms restricted her movements.

"Put me down."

"No."

"Where are you taking me?"

"Out of this blizzard."

"Why?"

"Would you prefer to stay in the snow and freeze?" Kayla felt a poke in her ribs from his thick finger. "Seems to me you wouldn't last two hours out here."

"I can take care of myself."

"Oh can you now?" The man's laughter shook Kayla as she rested over his shoulder. She glanced about trying to place where she was, in order to make an escape later, but all she could see was white.

"Follow the tracks," Kayla said to herself as she stared at the man's footprints left in the snow. "Idiot, with the snowing coming down, those will be gone in a few hours. Think Kayla. Landmarks, shadows, anything."

Kayla lifted her head up trying to find something that she could use as a compass should she get free from her captors. But the white drifting snow gave nothing away, and she knew she would get lost and probably freeze just as they predicted. For now, she was going to have to play nice.

In the distance, Kayla could see small lights coming out of the snowy field. She kept her eyes open and her guard up as she was brought down the slope to a small village.

"Jessie," The first man stopped at the edge of the forest and waited for Jessie to catch up. "Take her to Alice and get her warmed up. She has some explaining to do."

"Alice isn't going to like a stranger in her home."

"I know, but where else could we leave her?" Nate nodded to Kayla and she saw a hint of disgust in his eyes. Kayla couldn't help but grunt and shake her head as the brute carried her down to the first little house in the village.

The knock on the door startled Kayla, but she tried not to jump. It was only when she heard the soft female chime, ringing from the other side of the door, did she realize she was being passed on to another.

"Hello?" the woman answered the door in a pleasant tone. "Jessie. What can I do for you tonight?"

"Nate wants you to hold on to this for tonight."

"Does he now? Well, tell Nate that I am not a baby sitter."

"Alice." Jessie's voice dropped and Kayla could imagine his eyes narrowing on the poor girl.

"Fine, put it on the couch."

"I am not an *it*." Kayla snapped as Jessie walked into the house, passing Alice in the doorway. Jessie shook his head as he plopped Kayla down onto the couch.

"Stay put little girl if you know what's best for you." Jessie's eyebrows pulled together as he shook his finger at her. Kayla crossed her arms and stuck out her tongue.

"She's got spunk. I like her." Alice chimed in as Jessie stomped through the house and disappeared behind the door as Alice closed it.

"Well, for the record, I'm Alice." The small tiny-framed woman walked over to Kayla with her hand extended and a smile stretching across her face. For a moment Kayla hesitated to shake her hand, but hadn't been Alice who had kidnapped her.

"I'm Kayla."

"Well, Kayla, it would seem you got lucky out there tonight, when the boys found you."

"Oh really? Well if they weren't gallivanting in the street, I wouldn't have needed their assistance."

Alice laughed as she walked over to the large fireplace and pulled a match from a container. She struck the match and threw it into the pile of wood. In an instant, the little house was filled with warmth and light. Kayla's eyes popped as she noticed the long scars running down Alice's face.

"Don't worry, I am used to people staring."

"How?" The question caught Alice off guard and she pressed her lips into a tight line, wondering how to answer. Kayla watched as Alice struggled with the right words.

"There are creatures in these woods that don't take kindly to strangers. I got caught in the wrong place at the wrong time."

"Did they do that to you?" Kayla pointed to the door as heat sparked in her. She began to wonder how hard it would be to take out the brutes who had plucked her from her truck. She knew the two of them were strong, but would she be able to inflict damage if it came down to it? As Kayla tried to figure out her battle plan, Alice laughed. The sound filled the small space of the living room. Kayla glanced at Alice wondering what was so funny.

"I can see you working yourself up over there," Alice said with a smile teasing the corner of her full lips. "But it wasn't them if that is what you were thinking. Those boys saved me from the wolves. You see, sometimes legends and myths are true."

"Telling stories again, Alice?"

Kayla's eyes darted to the door, where Nate stood. He pulled back his thick heavy coat and shook the snow from it before stepping inside.

"When am I not?"

"Don't listen to her. She likes to scare people." Nate said as Kayla scooted to the furthest corner of the couch.

"I am not scared of wolves or bears, or anything else that roams wild." Kayla stated as she kept her eyes locked on Nate.

"Really?" The way Nate's voice rose to the challenge wasn't something Kayla was anticipating, but she held her place waiting for him to strike.

"Here's the deal. Your truck is pretty badly damaged. I'm surprised you survived wrapping it around that tree. You are going to have to stay here a few days so that the mechanic can fix it up."

"Are you keeping me here? Or can I leave at any time?" Nate's eyes narrowed in on Kayla as she asked her question.

"You are free to go whenever you'd like, but that storm isn't lifting anytime soon. You might as well get comfortable here. And since we don't have hotels anywhere in the village, you are going to have to bunk here with Alice."

Nate glanced at Alice and she nodded obediently. Kayla's eyes flickered to the tiny woman with her long raven-black hair, before she turned back towards Nate.

"Look, I am sorry that I caused you to crash. I should have been paying attention to where I was. The least I can do is to offer you a place to stay and to fix your truck. If you feel uneasy here, there are other places you can stay. But like I said, we don't have hotels."

"How long?" Kayla's jaw clamped down as she contemplated her choices.

"A few days, tops. Who knows, maybe the storm will let up by the time your truck is ready."

Kayla glanced at Alice once again. The smile on the girl's face appeared genuine, stretching to her eyes. Kayla nodded despite the uneasy sensation growing in the back of her mind.

"A few days, and then I'm gone."

"It's settled then." Alice clapped her hands as Nate plopped down on the couch beside Kayla.

"I don't think I introduced myself earlier, I'm Nate."

"Kayla."

"That's an interesting name."

"Is it? Never occurred to me." Kayla kept her distance as Alice stroked the fire.

"Don't you want to get warmed up by the fire?" Nate suggested as the flames licked the dry wood.

"The cold doesn't really bother me."

Nate and Alice exchanged glances and Kayla noticed the unspoken exchange between the two of them. She held her tongue and waited for one of them to break the silence first. She could tell it was going to be a long two days if everyone in the village was like this.

"You don't have to be scared of us," Nate said finally. "We won't hurt you."

"I doubt you could, even if you wanted to." Nate's eyes widened as Kayla's words left her mouth.

"I wouldn't be so bold if I were you. You have no idea what we are capable of."

"And you shouldn't under estimate me." Kayla glared at Nate, hoping the fire in her eyes burned with the warning in her voice. Nate chuckled as he tilted his head. Again, Kayla sensed a conversation between Nate and

Alice and she turned to face the fire. It had been a long day, but even so, she wasn't about to sleep here with so much going on.

"Alice, why don't you get our new friend here a drink? Make it a strong one. She needs to relax."

"Sure thing." With that, Alice skipped out of the living room and disappeared behind the corner leaving Kayla alone with Nate.

"I know what you are thinking," Nate finally said. "And you are wrong. We won't hurt you."

"How do you know what I am thinking?"

"Your eyes give you away. But rest easy. You will be on your way soon enough. And with time and luck, you will forget about this place."

"Hey, what did I miss?" The door flew open and Kayla's eyes darted to the thick heavy set man in the doorway.

"Adam, meet Kayla. She will be joining our little tribe for a few days."

"She the one who ran you over?" Adam laughed as he stomped into the house leaving the door wide open.

"Close the door!" Alice scolded from the kitchen. "You may not mind the cold, but I do."

"Sorry." Adam quickly retreated back to the door and closed it.

"Kayla, this is Adam."

"So, this little thing almost killed you and you bring her here?"

"I think you got the facts wrong. I almost killed her and yes. I brought her here to make sure she was okay."

"Does Jessie know?"

"He was the one who carried her back."

"Alrighty then," Adam flashed a brilliant smile towards Kayla as Alice came back into the living room holding cups.

"Don't I get one?" Adam asked as he stole Alice's chair while she passed out the drinks.

"You know where the kitchen is, get it yourself."

Kayla couldn't help but laugh as Adam huffed and mumbled under his breath. For a moment she understood the tension she felt was of her own making. It had Been far too long since she had been around any real families and she had forgotten what they were like. Alice gave Kayla her glass with a smile and a nod. Kayla glanced at the brown liquid before taking a whiff of what it might be.

"Don't worry, I will tell you if she poisoned you," Nate said with a chuckle and tapped his nose.

"I would never." Alice scoffed as she handed Nate his glass before turning to Adam in anticipation. Alice tapped her foot waiting for Adam to move.

Kayla giggled as Adam pulled himself out of the chair allowing Alice to reclaim it.

"Fine, I will get my own. But don't think I won't forget this Alice."

"Bottoms up," Alice said raising her glass up into the air. Kayla waited for the others to down their glasses before taking a swig. The caramel colored liquid burned as it trickled down her throat. Nate's eyes lingered on Kayla as she finished the shot. From the corner, Kayla could feel Adam's eyes on her as well, waiting for something to happen.

Kayla set her glass down and stared at them.

"Alice, maybe you could loan Kayla some clothes to wear? She may not mind the cold, but frost bite is not a pretty sight and I would hate for her to lose her nose."

"Sure thing Nate, come on Kayla. You can pick anything you want. I am sure you wouldn't mind a hot shower either."

"Thanks." Kayla set the small glass down and rose from the couch.

"When you are done, maybe you can answer a few questions for us?"

"Like what?" Kayla turned to Nate, her guard up once again.

"Where you are going? Where you came from? News from beyond the mountain."

"We don't get cable out here and I have been dying to know what is happening with the Bachelor. Did he pick a wife yet?" Alice's questions threw Kayla for a loop. Kayla's eyebrows rose as she chuckled and shook her head. Kayla opened her mouth to answer, but was cut off.

"Get comfortable first," Nate said. "Then we will talk."

"Come on, let me show you around."

With that, Alice grabbed Kayla by the hand and led her upstairs to the bathroom.

"Take your time. I am sure; you will want a few moments alone. When you are done, just go into my closet and find something to wear."

"Thank you," Kayla said as Alice closed the bathroom door giving Kayla the much needed space she had always loved so much.

Chapter 3

Kayla pulled her shirt over her head and stared at herself in the bathroom mirror. A single bruise striped down her shoulder to her chest, from the seatbelt that had restrained her during the crash. As she was staring at it, the angry purple bruise faded to a soft yellow before disappearing into her regular skin tone.

Kayla panted as she slumped down to the sink. The stress of healing her body took more out of her than she expected. She steadied herself and reached into the basin of the tub, pulling the knob to start the water of the shower. She continued to strip and stepped into the hot water. The moment she submerged her head, all her troubles vanished. Kayla couldn't remember the last time she had such a leisurely shower. Normally, her showers were in the public showers and were quick with several pairs of eyes on her. Here, she relished the fact she was completely alone. If it weren't for the hushed, whispered going on downstairs, she would have stayed in there longer. But something Nate said caught her attention.

"I don't think she knows." Nate's voice carried through the vent into the bathroom setting Kayla on edge.

"Doesn't matter. She might be the one he has been hunting the past twenty years."

"Are we really going to hand her over, just like that?" Nate's voice sounded pained, almost weary as he spoke. Kayla kept the water running as she leaned closer to the vent hoping to get more information. She knew that if she let the water stop, they would hear it and she wasn't finished eavesdropping.

"Why? What is she to you?" Kayla heard Jessie's voice crack, and she wondered who they were setting her up to meet.

"I'm telling you, she is just a girl in the wrong place at the wrong time. We shouldn't pull her into this."

"But what if she is exactly whom we have been looking for?" Adam's voice rose above the hushed whispers.

"All the more reason for us to protect her," Nate said in a stern protective voice.

"Sounds to me you got a little crush going on." Jessie teased. For a moment Kayla thought of the kindness in Nate's eyes as he pulled from the wreckage. The idea of being with anyone shook her to her core. She knew that anyone she got close to would end up getting hurt and she couldn't do that to these people. She shook her head and turned off the water. There was no way she wanted to hear Nate's response. Her heart couldn't take it.

"Shh. Listen." Kayla heard Alice's voice clearly through the vent, as she wrapped the towel around her waist and knew she was smart to have left it running while she listened in on them. "She's out of the shower."

"I'm going to go get him." Jessie said and Nate hushed him.

"Don't you dare."

"Might as well get it over with. It's not like she is going to be kept a secret in this village. Besides, he probably already knows."

"Jessie is right Nate. Let Jessie bring him here and we can figure out what to do afterwards." Adam whispered and Kayla sucked in a deep breath. Drops of water dripped from her wet hair and sounded like knocking on the door. Kayla rung out her hair and stepped out of the bathroom prepared for anything.

"I'm at least going to warn her before you go. I would hate to put her in an uncomfortable situation. I mean she has probably already snuck out of the bathroom window by now." Nate's voice strained, but Kayla could hear him as if he stood right beside her.

"I'll go with Jessie," Adam announced and the springs from the couch squeaked from the pressure of his movements.

"Alice, prepare the house. You are about to have guests."

"What are you going to do?" Alice asked as Kayla stood listening at the top of the stairs.

"Kayla has the right to know what's happening. She may not have hit me, but James will not see it that way. Better make sure the girl can handle the fire before we throw her into it."

Kayla stepped away from the stairwell and snuck back into the bedroom. There, she scrambled to the closet and grabbed a shirt and pants. Although the clothes weren't hers, they felt strangely familiar. Maybe Alice was her size after all.

Kayla didn't flinch as Nate rapped on the bedroom door. She twisted her head to see him standing in the doorway as she lifted the shirt to her head.

"You can come in," Kayla stated hoping that whatever was really going on, she could use her body to get her out of the danger. She paused with the shirt just over her head waiting for the door to click before she fully exposed herself to Nate. Nate stepped through and saw her half-naked in the room. His eyes widened as Kayla continued to pull the top down over her body.

"Wait." Nate said as he covered the space between them in two wide strides. Kayla tried to hide her smile as she felt Nate's fingers graze over her shoulder blades lifting the shirt back up.

"Can I help you?" Kayla asked waiting for Nate to give her some space to pull her shirt back down, but he held it up refusing to let her put it on.

"How did you get this mark?" Nate traced the scar on her shoulder blade, sending chills racing under Kayla's skin. A smiled played at the corner of Nate's lips as he watched the goose bumps rise on Kayla's skin. Kayla shivered involuntary as Nate's fingers glided down her spine from the scar. The moment Nate's finger left her body; she pulled the shirt down covering her body.

"I've had it for as long as I can remember, why?"

Kayla tried not to let her words drift, but Nate was so close she could feel the heat from his breath as he spoke. Nate stared at her as he pulled up his shirt revealing his chiseled body. Kayla's lips pulled at the corners as she studied him. Everything from his kind soft eyes down to his trim body tickled her fancy. Although she was about to use her sex appeal to intimidate Nate, she suddenly found herself on the receiving end.

"Don't let him do this to you," she said to herself as Nate turned. Even his back was ripped. Kayla stared at his smooth strong back and wondered how strong he really was as his muscles stretched. Nate twisted his head around to glance at Kayla before rubbing a small mark on his neck.

"You see that?" Nate pointed to the gap between his shoulders and neck. Kayla stole a step forward. There by the light of the room, she noticed the marking on him.

"That is the same one I have. But …?"

"Not exactly the same."

"So? What does this mean?" Kayla traced the lines of Nate's back as the electricity flowed through her fingers. She allowed the sensation to overcome her senses. The pull to Nate was astonishing. Never before had the center of her being wanted something so badly.

"I don't know." Nate let the words linger on the air between them. Kayla wondered if he was drawn to her as well as she dropped her fingers. Nate turned around and looked at her. In his eyes was the same fire that burned in Kayla's. Nate stepped closer.

"It's just unusual, that's all. I haven't seen one like that in a really long time."

"Ok-a-ay." Kayla let the word linger on the air as she turned away and reached for the light jacket hanging in the closet. Nate's hand stretched out and touched hers before she could pull the jacket from the hanger.

"Where are you going?" Nate asked wrapping his fingers around Kayla's wrist and spun her back around. Before Kayla could protest, Nate's lips crushed hers. While Nate's tongue parted Kayla's lips, to open her up, her fingers were hungrily groping Nate's body forcing him closer. All she wanted right then and there as to be swallowed by Nate. Every inch of her being craved him like oxygen. She had to have him and she didn't care who walked in. She closed her eyes allowing the animal rattling its cage to be released.

Kayla pushed Nate away from her, throwing him down to the bed. With a smile on his face, Nate climbed to the edge and reached for Kayla's clothes. As he rose, Nate pulled Kayla's shirt off her, exposing her perfect round breasts. He opened his mouth wide and tugged on Kayla to come closer. She giggled as Nate's tongue circled her hardened nipple, taking all he could. Kayla mounted Nate causing the mattress to groan under their weight. The sound startled Kayla. She opened her eyes and pulled away.

"I can't do this."

"Why not? What's wrong?"

"I just can't." Kayla stated as Nate continued to pursue her. His hands raced down her bare back and grabbed her ass. His fingers hooked into her butt cheeks like the talons of an eagle scooping up a fish from the waters. She knew there was no way she was going to get out of his clutches and, deep down, she didn't want to.

"Don't pull away now. You want this, I know you do."

Chapter 4

Nate allowed one hand to linger on Kayla's butt, keeping her mounted on him as the other slipped between her legs and pulled the zipper of her pants down. Kayla's eyes flickered down to watch as Nate's fingers undid the button of her pants. With a sigh, Kayla allowed herself to swim in the lust that surrounded them.

Nate pressed his lips between Kayla's breasts as his hand worked down towards her crotch making Kayla lose her resolve. It wasn't until she heard a giggle behind her that Kayla stopped. Whipping her head around, she saw Alice standing in the doorway, observing Nate's attempt to bed her.

"Alice!"

"Don't mind her," Nate mumbled as his fingers drifted further down.

"But, this is so wrong."

"It's not wrong if it feels so right." Nate twisted his head around Kayla's body and winked at Alice. The petite girl strolled into the room, discarding her clothes as she moved closer. Kayla's heart drummed in her chest as she watched Alice undress. The female body always thrilled Kayla despite the fact that she loved men too much to commit fully.

Nate pressed his tongue over Kayla's nipples as Alice grazed her fingers over Kayla's back. The heat from Alice's body against Kayla's soothed her fears. Only when Alice pressed her breasts into Kayla's back, did Kayla dive in head first.

Nate's tongue grazed over Kayla's breasts licking one, then the other. Alice kept her hands on Kayla's back forcing her to stay. It was only when Nate reached Kayla's moist cotton panties, did she realize that she wanted this too much to say no now. Chills raced through her as she gasped for air. She closed her eyes allowing Nate's hand to drop further down.

"Put her on the bed," Alice groaned. "I want to watch her expression as you fill her."

Alice stepped back allowing Nate to slip his hand back out of Kayla's pants and he wrapped them around her waist. In one fluid motion, Kayla was turned around and landed softly on the mattress with Nate hovering above her.

Alice stood to the side of him with her wild eyes locked on Kayla.

Inch by inch he pulled down Kayla's pants until they were bunched at her ankles. Her eyes rolled back as Nate dove to the space between her legs and she sighed. His hot breath tickled her slit through the cotton fabric of her panties as he breathed on her, teasing her. His hands dropped to Kayla's ankles releasing her pants before throwing them over his head.

With one hand Kayla reached out for the wall to brace herself, as Nate's fingers played with the elastic binding of her underwear. There was no turning back now. Nate was too close to getting what he wanted, and Kayla body craved his touch. She sucked in air through her nose as Nate's fingers pulled back the cotton panties and she felt the wet caress of his tongue.

"Nate," she huffed as her hands reached down to his head buried between her legs.

"Mmm," he moaned as his finger slipped into her body. Kayla's knees began to shake and her eyes darted to Alice. Alice stared at them with wide, eager eyes, inching forward onto the bed. Her breasts bounced up and down as she struggled to get closer.

"I think there is someone else who wants to play."

Nate emerged from between Kayla's legs with juices covering his face. Kayla had hoped he would pull his fingers from her body to release her, but they remained rubbing against her inner walls.

"She won't go far," he noted as he rose. His fingers twitched within Kayla spreading her open as he scooted next to Kayla nibbling on her neck with his eyes locked on Alice.

"Besides, she is only here to watch."

"What?" Alice cried out trying to get between Nate and Kayla.

"You heard me," Nate shot her a glance that shut her up. "Now be a good little girl and let Daddy play with his new toy."

Nate turned his attention back to Kayla. "Come Kayla," Nate said keeping his fingers locked inside of her like a hook dragging her towards the back wall. "Alice has been a naughty little girl, and she needs a time out."

"Nate, I don't..." his fingers pressed against Kayla's lips silencing her. He shook his head and leaned into her. His hard erection throbbed against Kayla's thighs itching to enter something wet.

"Shh, don't speak. Just let go and enjoy yourself. You can't hurt us, I promise."

"But," Kayla began as Nate pulled his fingers from her making sure to rub Kayla's juices over every inch of her pussy. Without thinking about it, Kayla spun around to face the back wall and bent over sticking her ass in the air. With her head down, she waited.

Alice snickered as Nate moved behind Kayla. His hands drifted down Kayla's bare back and over her cotton panties.

"Give it to her," Alice squealed as Nate pulled Kayla's underwear off to one side exposing the swollen lips of her pussy between her thighs. Nate's fingers ran over Kayla's slit as she dug her fingers into the lush comforter beneath her.

With one hand Nate positioned his prick between Kayla's thighs and pressed his body to her.

"Oh God," Kayla gasped as the head of his cock penetrated her. The cotton underwear chaffed the sides of Kayla's vagina as he began pounding his body into hers. As their hips collided and crashed against one another, Kayla tried to remain focused. She knew that if she let the animal out, bad things would happen. But with each thrust, Nate's cock dug deeper into her. With every inch of his dick that slipped into her, Kayla lost a little more of her resolve. Before she could stop herself, she began pushing her body back into his, begging for more.

The crack of his hand on Kayla's rear end added the spice she needed. The mark on her ass only intensified Nate's desires as he raised his other hand and sent it crashing down to the other side of her body.

"Don't move," he ordered as Kayla continued to push back into him taking as much of him as she could. Again, another slap as she moved.

"Don't hurt her," Alice begged as Nate's spanking grew harder, causing Kayla's skin to turn an angry red.

"She likes it."

Kayla bit down into the blanket to stifle her moans, as Nate rammed his hard cock into her. She opened her eyes and peeked between her legs. Something about watching a cock slid in and out always got Kayla's juices flowing. Every time he pulled his dick from her, she saw the white bodily fluid of her pussy dripping down his shaft. Using one hand to keep herself propped up, Kayla slipped the other between her legs and latched on to his shaft as he moved.

The pressure of Kayla's fingers around his cock caused Nate to moan. His hands grabbed her sides as his speed intensified. The slapping of their bodies filled the room as their juices mingled.

"God, woman," Nate cooed as he pulled out of Kayla abruptly. "You are going to make me come."

"I thought that was the idea," she teased as she glanced over her shoulder. Kayla's eyes darted to Alice sitting and waiting patiently beside them. A smile played at the corner of Kayla's lips as Alice rubbed the tiny bulb between her legs. The lust in her eyes pleaded for Kayla to let her play.

"You don't get my cum," Nate said stumbling back. "She does."

Kayla shifted her body around as Nate moved to Alice. With his cock in his hand, Nate stroked the length of it and placed his dick just far enough away from Alice's face that only the very tip of her tongue could reach it.

"You want this don't you?" Nate teased as Alice's tongue stretched out to lick the crown. Kayla plopped down on the bed with her eyes locked on Alice. The absence of Nate's rod in her caused her pussy to swell. Kayla sat back and opened her legs wide allowing Alice and Nate full access to how she liked to play. With one hand Kayla reached down and began rubbing her juices over her pussy soaking her panties in the process.

Alice's eyes darted to Kayla as she rubbed her clit and slipped two fingers into her opening. Moaning as Kayla entered herself, Alice smiled. Nate's eyes shifted to Kayla as he took a scoot closer to Alice. Alice clasped her mouth around Nate's head. The slurping noise of Alice sucking tickled Kayla as she kept her fingers in herself and began thrusting in and out to satisfy the emptiness Nate had left.

Kayla's chest rose and fell as her eyes lingered on Alice's tight lips surrounding Nate's thick hard cock. Every so often Kayla would glance at Nate. With his back arched, one hand on his hips, he pushed his rod further into Alice's mouth. Alice gagged as Nate slid his cock down to the back of her throat and back out again. Nate kept one hand on his thick shaft ensuring that every time his head popped out of Alice's wet mouth, his cock was right there to re-enter her again.

"Please, let me play" Alice choked as Nate fucked her face. Images of Alice attacking Nate played in Kayla's mind as she circled around the folds of her vagina tickling her labia with each pass. The hidden bud swelled as Kayla played, reminding her of the lack of attention she was getting.

Pulling her fingers from her crotch, Kayla scooted to the edge of the bed and stood.

"Just what do you think you are doing?" Nate barked as Kayla moved around the bed and stood behind him.

"Taking what I want," Kayla said as her hands circled his hips until her breasts pressed against his back. Kayla's hands slipped around Nate's and he pulled them back allowing Kayla to replace his, around his cock. Kayla squeezed as hard as she could until he groaned.

"Do you like tight pussies?" Kayla whispered in Nate's ear purposefully grazing her teeth against his flesh.

"The tighter the better."

With a flick of Kayla's wrists, her hand moved down Nate's shaft until her little finger grazed over the stubble on his balls. With another twist, Kayla jerked her hand back up. Alice's saliva covered the length of him making it smoother for Kayla to do what she wanted to do to him. Alice's mouth drew him in as Kayla's hand pulled him out again. Kayla leaned up against Nate's shoulder brushing her lips against his neck and shoulders. Kayla's hot breath on Nate sent his body into convulsions.

"Enough," he pleaded as Kayla increased the speed. Nate shifted his body back plucking his cock out of the vacuum that was Alice's mouth. Kayla stumbled as Nate moved trying to keep her body as close to his as possible.

"That's it; get your ass to the bed now."

"Make me." Kayla glared at Nate holding her ground. With a twisted little smile, Nate stepped in closer.

Chapter 5

Nate wrestled with Kayla's body as she squirmed about, making it difficult for him to get a solid grip around her frame. Laughter overtook Kayla as Nate wound his arms around her waist picking her up off the floor and carried her around the bed to the open spot on the other side. Kayla landed hard on the soft mattress with her face planted in the crack between two pillows as her ass stuck out into the air.

"You are not playing nice," Nate huffed as Kayla giggled.

"I never do."

"Good, it's no fun when they play nice," Nate groaned as his eyes shifted to Alice before allowing the crown of his cock to teased the lips of Kayla's pussy searching for a way in. The moment he penetrated Kayla, her body arched. Nate's dick filled her as the walls of her body tightened. With each thrust, he pushed the air from Kayla's lungs causing her to moan as she tried to regain the expelled air. The harder he pounded, the more difficult it became for Kayla to keep a clear head.

Nate wrapped his fingers around Kayla's neck and squeezed, cutting off what little air she managed to steal between his blows.

"Now you are going to sit here like a good little girl," Nate's voice broke with each syllable as he buried himself further into Kayla than ever before. The moment his hands released Kayla, she pulled in a deep breath clearing the fog from her sight.

"No," she managed to shout as Kayla twisted her head around to glare at him. Sweat dripped from his forehead as his cock swelled inside of Kayla stretching her more than before.

"What did you say?"

"I didn't stutter. I am not Alice. You won't find me as an easy target."

"Hey," Alice protested as Nate's head whipped around.

"Be quiet," Nate ordered Alice. "If you know what's good for you."

"But," Alice started. Nate pulled his cock from Kayla as he pushed her down into the bed. He turned and faced Kayla with a wicked smile.

"You will stay right there."

"Or what?" Kayla's eyes narrowed challenging Nate's order.

His hand came up and crashed down on Kayla's bare ass. Pain shot through her offsetting the pleasure.

"Ouch."

"I will spank you harder next time. Now, do as I say."

"For now," Kayla cooed as she rubbed the sting away.

Nate shifted his attention back to Alice. His tight brown ass flexed as he walked away from Kayla. Kayla stayed put running her hands over the course of her body as he drew closer to Alice.

"Lick her juices off me." Nate shoved his cock into Alice's mouth. The way she devoured him thrilled Kayla. Alice's tongue moved over his flesh as if it was her last meal. Kayla's eyes widened as Alice swallowed Nate whole, savoring every bit of him. Nate's eyes closed as Alice drew back until only the crown of his cock was engulfed by her lips.

Kayla slipped her hand between her legs and caressed her clit waiting for Nate's return. When Alice pushed the cock out of her mouth, Nate's eyes popped open.

"You are such a tease."

"You like it like that," Alice smirked as Nate leaned down and pressed his lips to hers.

"Get next to Kayla, I want both your asses in the air."

Alice didn't hesitate, she scrambled over the bed and joined Kayla on the other side.

"Do you always do what you are told?" Kayla asked Alice as the girl inched herself as close to the edge as she could, waiting for Nate. Alice's eyes darted to Kayla as Nate's footsteps drew closer.

"Alice is a good little girl, unlike you."

"You need a bad girl every now and again. Or is that why you resorted to running people off the road? The passion died, and you needed something to spice it up a bit?"

Nate's hand went up and crashed down on Kayla's ass. Alice winced as she heard the crack and glanced at Kayla's burning butt cheek. Kayla didn't make a sound as she remained hunch over the edge of the bed.

"Oh, my," Alice's eyes drifted back to Kayla as Kayla stared at the pillows. "Are you okay?"

"She's fine," Nate answered as his hands grasped Kayla's hips. With Alice's saliva dripping from his cock, he shoved into Kayla, only then did she whimper. With the added weight from Alice, the bed squeaked and moaned as Nate rammed Kayla harder.

Nate's fingers dug into Kayla's flesh as the walls of her pussy swelled from the attention. Kayla's body drew taut as her juices spilled out of her. Alice's eyes were on Nate and Kayla as Nate's balls slammed against Kayla's ass. With one hand Kayla reached down between Alice's legs and caressed her clit. With each thrust, Kayla pressed against Alice's little bulb, hidden between her pussy lips. As Alice's pussy ached, Kayla slipped her fingers deeper into Alice.

"Oh my God," Alice squealed as Kayla rammed her with two fingers and managed to shove a third into her hot little body. Alice's hips wiggled and squirmed as Kayla rubbed her down. Deep within her, Kayla hit Alice's g-spot with the very tip of her middle finger.

"Holy shit." Alice's head went down into the pillow as Kayla continued to play with her. Each time Nate's cock slipped out of Kayla, she wondered if and when Nate would shift to Alice. There was, after all, only one reason for the both Alice and Kayla to be on the bed side by side. Nate wanted them both.

"That's enough out of you," Nate said leaning over Kayla. His sweaty chest made his body slippery as he glided over Kayla's body and reached for her swollen nipples. As he pinched them between his thumb and pointer finger, Kayla yelped.

"I'm not done with you yet, so stay wet for me."

"Maybe I will just have to finish myself off." Kayla struggled to force the words out as she sucked in the clean air she so desperately needed.

"Don't you dare."

Nate sidestepped bringing Alice to his hips. Kayla's fingers remained in Alice dancing about her insides.

Through a small space between Kayla's fingers, Nate pushed his cock into Alice.

"Ahh," she growled as Kayla refused to leave her and with Nate shoving his way deeper into her. Kayla glanced over her shoulder to stare at Nate as he retracted his cock before pounding and crashing his hips into Alice's.

"You are in my way," Nate sneered as Alice grunted and dug her fingers into the soft pillows at her head.

"I was here first." Kayla grumbled digging her fingers deeper into Alice. Alice shifted her hips down forcing Kayla's fingers to go deeper.

"Move." Nate warned thrusting his cock into the small space.

"No." Kayla argued as she wiggled her fingers around Nate's cock while it throbbed inside Alice.

"Please," Alice panted. "Stay. Both. Of. You."

The sensation of being stretched must have been the kind of attention Alice had been craving. As Nate resumed his position and shoved his dick through Kayla's fingers, Kayla wiggled around his wet slippery shaft. Kayla's eyes darted to Alice as her mouth opened wider and wider. With Alice's eyes shut tight, she endured the pressure.

Deep within her body, Alice's muscles began to tighten around Kayla's fingers. As space grew smaller and smaller, Kayla pulled her fingers out giving Nate the needed room to do what he did best. Kayla painted her opening and clit with Alice's dripping juices.

"You come for me," Nate huffed as he increased his speed. The bed rocked as Nate shoved into Alice with violent intent. Kayla pushed back trying to keep the bed from rocking Nate and Alice fucked beside her. With Kayla's pussy aching for attention, she pulled her hand away from Alice.

"No," Alice bleated.

"I need attention too."

Alice wiggled her arm out from under her body and drifted it down between Kayla's legs. As Alice tried to find Kayla's center, her nails grazed over Kayla's thighs.

"Stop," Kayla clasped her hand around Alice's and pulled Alice's hand back. It was clear Alice was far too involved with Nate to be paying any attention to Kayla's needs.

"But," she huffed as Alice retracted her arm. Alice's face turned a darker shade of red.

"That's my good little slut, cum all over me."

As Kayla's juices poured out of her, her breathing intensified. Her lungs begged for fresh air as she dropped her head into the pillow to stifle her moans. On the edge of coming, Kayla held back trying to focus on something else. She didn't have to wait long before Nate pulled out.

Alice's juices flowed out of her body, covering Nate's bright red cock. A smile played at the corner of Kayla's lips as she reached for his scrotum. With his balls in Kayla's fingers, she rolled them around in their tight little sack.

"Ooohh," Nate huffed trying to keep the momentum going as Alice crumbled into the bed, spent. Standing straight, Nate remained in Alice but stopped moving. Kayla's body reacted with the knowledge that Nate was throbbing in Alice to extend her orgasm.

"How do you feel?" he asked as Alice bit her bottom lip. With droopy eyes, she stared at Kayla. For a moment Kayla wondered if she even saw her through Alice's daze or if everything had faded to black.

"Mmm." Alice moaned reaching out towards Kayla. Alice's hand slipped from Kayla's body as Nate plucked his cock from her.

"Care to finish me off?"

Kayla glanced at his erection. The tip of his head burned red as the veins in his shaft pulsed for more.

"Do I have a choice?"

"Of course not."

Nate stepped over as Kayla twisted her body around. The soft cushions sank under Kayla's weight as Nate lifted her legs up over his shoulders. Kayla's eyes darted to his engorged cock as he plunged it into her. Kayla threw her head back as Nate pushed Alice's juices into Kayla's body.

"I love your tight pussy."

"You know how to make it tighter," Kayla said slipping her hand down. As Kayla rubbed her clit Nate's hand drifted down her leg and over her stomach until it reached its final destination. With his fingers clamped around Kayla's swollen nipples, he twisted and pulled.

"Make me come," he groaned as Kayla squeezed the muscles tight around his cock before releasing the muscles. Every time Kayla applied the pressure, Nate groaned with pleasure. Kayla went harder and longer between squeezing. She began counting his movements to time when she should clamp down on him.

"More." The sound of Alice's raspy voice was unexpected. Nate and Kayla both glanced over as she crawled over Kayla's hips. Alice's wet tongue added to the slipperiness of Nate's cock as Alice lapped and tasted Nate and Kayla's bodily fluids.

"Oh shit. Oh shit. I'm going to..." Nate couldn't finish his sentence before he pulled out of Kayla. Alice giggled as Nate's white jizz sprayed out from his tip and drenched Kayla's face. Alice stuck out her tongue and opened her mouth to receive all she could from him.

Lying back, Kayla watched as Nate stroked Alice's hair while she licked every bit of the juices off Nate's cock. Only when Alice slurped up the last bit did Nate stumble back. Kayla's legs dropped to the ground, and she scooted back up to the wall of the bed panting.

"Two out of three," Nate whimpered as his chest rose and fell grabbing the air he needed. "Now it's your turn."

"Another time, you have company." Nate, Alice, and Kayla turned their attention to Jessie who stood in the open door way with eyes wide. The spark in his face told Kayla he wished he had stayed, but there were more pressing matters to deal with.

Kayla jumped off the bed and grabbed her clothes from the floor as Alice kept her eyes to the ground, with a beet-red face. Alice moved with haste, gathering what she needed as Jessie stood with his arms locked across his chest staring at her.

"Nate," Jessie's eye flickered to Nate as Nate casually snagged his pants and shoved past Jessie in the door way.

"Next time, you should go for someone with more stamina." Jessie winked at Kayla as she pulled her shirt on and slipped back into her pants. A smile played at the corner of Kayla's lips.

"This was a one-time thing," Kayla said as she grabbed Jessie's crotch on her way out the door.

"Sure it was," Jessie huffed as Alice tried to slip out the door. Jessie's hand went up blocking Alice.

"You know better."

"But they invited me." Alice kept her eyes down refusing to look at Jessie.

"Did they?" Jessie turned to glance at Kayla who blew him a kiss.

"A girl likes variety," Kayla answered as she disappeared down the steps.

It didn't take long for the euphoria to wear off. The moment Kayla reached the second step, all eyes were on her. She sucked in a deep breath as her eyes lingered over the crowd in the living room.

"So," an elderly man said as his eyes locked onto Kayla. "This is our guest, huh?"

Kayla recognized Nate and Adam, but the other two men standing beside the elder looked more like body guards than family. Kayla moved slowly down the last two steps before stopping at the base of the stairs.

"Please, have a seat. There is so much we need to talk about."

Chapter 6

"My name is Eric. I am the chief of this village."

"Hi," Kayla moved to the open chair and glanced around the room. From what she could tell by the others' expressions, she was not welcome. Only Nate's face showed signs of acceptance.

"My son," Eric gestured to Jessie before placing his hand down on the couch's armrest. "Tells me you nearly hit him, driving down the road."

"It wasn't like that," Kayla spouted as Jessie came down the stairs with Alice in tow. Eric's eyes shifted to Jessie who stepped around Kayla's chair to take his place next to his father.

"Yes, yes, the snow." Eric raised his hand cutting Kayla off. "It happens." Eric's lips twitched before his face turned to stone as if it was completely normal for his people to be run over.

"What I want to know is when you plan to leave."

"As soon as my truck is fixed," Kayla's eyes darted to Nate then Jessie. Jessie leaned down to his father and whispered in his ear. Eric nodded without saying a word as his eyes remained locked on Kayla.

"I see. So, in a few days?" Eric's lips pressed into a tight line as the others surrounding him began to murmur amongst themselves.

"Very well," the old man said as he rose from the couch. "You may stay for the two days that is required for your truck to be fixed. However," Eric paused glaring at Alice. "You will remain here. There is no reason for you to venture outside these four walls."

"Excuse me?" Kayla glared at Eric. Never before had she been refrained from the outdoors.

"It is for your safety that I request that you stay here."

"And what if I don't?" Kayla challenged. Eric's eyes narrowed on her as if somehow he was testing her will.

"Then I will not be responsible for what happens to you, my dear. The woods are filled with creatures that would love nothing more than to eat you up." Eric flashed his sharp white teeth at Kayla. His blazing white teeth looked sharper against the withered brown skin of an old man. For a moment Kayla wondered if she should heed his warning or take his words as a threat.

She rose from her seat and crossed her arms. "Not that I am not grateful for your hospitality, but I can't stay cooped up inside all day."

"Suit yourself." Eric nodded to Jessie who glanced at Kayla, then at Nate. Nate shook his head ever so slightly before giving a low rumble. Kayla's eyes flickered to them as Jessie and Nate exchanged unspoken words and she knew they were talking about her.

"If you don't mind," Kayla grunted, staring the boys down. "Talking about someone is rude. If you have something to say, say it out loud for everyone to hear."

All eyes flickered to Kayla as their mouths dropped. "You heard us?" Jessie asked as his eyes grew wider.

"It is hard not to. If you really think you are going to keep me under house arrest, you got another thing coming."

"But how?" Jessie's wild eyes shifted to Eric who appeared just as curious as the others did.

"How what?"

"How could you hear us?"

"I have ears you know." Kayla glanced at Nate who shook his head again as if she shouldn't say another word.

"But," Jessie began as Eric threw up his hand, stopping Jessie from saying another word.

"It seems this girl is more than just a mere visitor." Eric stepped closer to Kayla keeping his gaze on her as he moved around her.

Eric sniffed the air around Kayla causing the hair on the back of her neck to stand up. Kayla gritted her teeth trying not to move a muscle. She fought against her instinct to rip the old man's throat out, but every fiber in her body scratched and clawed to defend itself.

"Take her to the barn. It is a new moon tonight. Let's see how she does under those circumstances."

Before Kayla could say another word, six pairs of arms were around her.

"Put me down now." Kayla demanded and immediately the arms released her as if they had no choice but to obey her every command.

Eric's eyes widened with fear as he stared at Kayla. "It can't be."

"Dad?" Jessie was just as confused as Eric was and stepped away from Kayla.

"Leave us, now." Eric's order was swift, as everybody in Alice's little house headed for the door; everyone except for Kayla.

"I would prefer an audience. I say everyone can stay."

The group paused with their heads twisting and turning trying to figure out what was going on. Only Nate stood with a smile stretched across his face and nodded with triumph.

"You are making a grave mistake, little girl." Eric's voice was laced with threat as he stepped closer to Kayla.

"You are the one trying to put me under house arrest." Kayla crossed her arms and stared the old man down. In the pit of her gut she understood that the old man held no power over her. How it was that she had power over the others, she didn't know. Her insides flipped as her ego grew.

"Matt!" Eric shouted out the name as Kayla's eyes shifted to the crowd. The people parted as Matt walked towards Eric and Kayla. With his eyes to the ground Matt, bowed low.

"Escort this girl to the barn."

Kayla glared at Eric as Matt curled his arm around Kayla's and pulled her towards the door.

"Let go of me." Kayla demanded, but Matt did not release her so easily.

"This is not a punishment," Matt whispered. "It is for your own good."

Kayla thrashed about as Matt dragged her out Alice's front door and down the street of the village. In the center of town a large building stood with barred windows and chains around the doors.

"What the hell?" Kayla's eyes grew wide as Matt walked her towards the opening.

"Please," Matt said requesting her hands.

"What are you doing?"

"A precaution."

"From what?" she asked.

Matt's eyes locked onto Kayla's as he bound her to the stake in the center of the barn. "You."

Chapter 7

Matt clamped the chains around Kayla's ankles and left her standing in the center of the barn alone. Kayla glanced around, waiting for someone to come to help her, but as the hours passed, she realized Eric must have ordered the others to stay away.

"Well, this is just great," Kayla grumbled glancing at the thick steel chains binding her to the wooden post. Fear gripped her heart stealing the warmth of her blood as the sun drifted below the horizon.

The shadows grew long as the night came. With no moon to give off light, Kayla was trapped in the darkness. Every nerve in her body fired off, as unusual sounds ripped through the village. Snarls and the gnashing of teeth echoed around her. Kayla braced herself for the worst, as several attacks on the barn doors sent the chains crashing against the wood.

"Leave me alone!" Kayla cried out in a strong voice. The charges to the barn door ceased. Only the ear-splitting howls of the creatures of the night caused her to shiver. Kayla sucked in a deep breath waiting for another onslaught, but when dawn's rays peeked through the cracks of the barn doors, she knew she was safe.

The lack of blood in her hands caused them to tingle, and she wondered how long they were going to keep her locked up in there. The only thing she could think to do would be to pick the locks. Unfortunately, she didn't know how. All she could do was thrash about until someone released her.

The creak of the barn door opening sent light flooding into the open space of the barn. Kayla squinted trying to get a good shot of who came in. She sucked in a deep breath waiting for the bullet to end her life.

"You made it through the night." Nate's voice surprised her as he walked up to her and released her from the chains. The other villagers stood around just outside the doors.

"What the hell," Kayla gasped ripping her arms away from Nate. "You people are seriously fucked up you know that?"

"Maybe, but you are one of us too you know."

"I am nothing like you." Kayla said as she rubbed her wrists allowing blood to flow freely through them once more.

"Clearly." Nate said with a smile. "Or you would have gotten loose last night."

"What?"

"Don't you know what you are?" Nate asked as Kayla stormed out of the barn with him on her heels.

"Pissed off is what I am." Kayla's eyes darted to the crowd of people circling the barn.

"You are a wolf, Kayla." Nate stated matter-of-factly. "Only you are special. One that isn't forced to change at the new moon."

"You are crazy. You know that right? Completely out of your mind."

"Think about it Kayla, why else are you attracted to me? You can feel it in your core. Why else didn't you hurt me yesterday, during sex?"

Kayla stopped dead in her tracks. Her eyes widened as she pondered on Nate's words. The last time she had had sex, she had nearly ripped the man to shreds. She had lost control. But, she didn't even scratch Nate or Alice. Kayla twisted on her heels and crossed her arms.

"How do you know about my escapades with others?"

"We all went through it at some point." Nate shifted to the crowd surrounding them. "We learn to control our animal instinct, but not indefinitely. We don't deny it though the way you do."

Kayla shook her head refusing to listen to anything else. She pushed her way through the bystanders, until she reached the edge of the forest. If she couldn't get back her truck, she was determined to walk until she reached civilization.

"You can't run from this!" Nate called after her. Kayla turned with a scowl.

"Let her go." Eric said with a smile stretched across his face. "She doesn't belong with us."

"But we can't let her go." Nate interjected as he kept his eyes locked on Kayla. Kayla stood at the edge of the forest contemplating her next move.

"She is a lone wolf. That is her choice. And no one here has the power to change her mind."

Kayla huffed as Eric finally said something she could agree with. She shook her head and pushed through the shrubs, walking until the village was far enough away that she knew the others wouldn't come after her.

"Stupid," Kayla said scolding herself as she stomped over the white-covered ground. "If only I'd have stayed at that stupid gas station. If I hadn't been so hasty, I would still have my truck and would probably be halfway to the ocean." Kayla pushed the low-hanging branches from her face as she continued forward.

"But you would have never met Nate," a softer voice said in her head. Kayla grunted.

"So what if I didn't hurt him? It was just sex, nothing more." Kayla said out loud trying to push the softer voice out of her head.

"Or maybe there is something to his words," the voice in her head cooed as Kayla climbed over a hill of snow and looked out towards the horizon.

Chapter 8

"Amazing isn't it?" The sound of Matt's voice startled her as she stared at the open snowy space before her. Kayla twisted her head and stared at Matt as he walked up to her and paused on the hill to take in the view.

"Are you here to bring me back?"

"No. But there is something I would like for you to see."

"It is the inside of another barn?" Kayla sneered as Matt shook his head and turned his back to the sun.

"There is something you need to see before you go. It is probably the reason you came back here to begin with."

"How can I come back to someplace, I have never been before?"

"But you have been here before." Matt paused, waiting for Kayla to follow him. "You were born here."

"What?" Kayla froze as she stared at Matt with wide eyes filled with wonder.

"You thought you were alone didn't you?" Matt's eyes softened and Kayla could see the years melting from him.

"I am alone."

"You don't have to be anymore. Please, let me explain." Matt opened his arm up gesturing for Kayla to follow. Curiosity nipped at her. She turned to the open forest once more before allowing herself to entertain the thought of a family.

"Fine, but after you show me what you are going to, can I leave?"

"I hope you will leave and forget this place."

"Why?"

"All in good time."

Matt strolled through the trees and Kayla followed. Neither speaking until they reached the edge of the forest. There a long river of black asphalt greeted them.

"You brought me to the road. Awesome. Thanks."

"That is not what you need to see." Matt pointed to the other side of the highway. There tucked under branches and surrounded by a pile of snow a cross rose up from the ground.

"That is where your parents died trying to protect you."

Kayla's eyes widened as she stared at the white cross that almost melted into the background. She shook her head as Matt walked down the steep embankment and crossed the road. For a moment Kayla wondered if she should follow or if she should allow Matt some time alone. After all, the cross could be for anyone and he was only making up that it was for her parents. Still, deep seated questions, which Kayla had long forgotten, rose to the surface of her mind.

"Alright, explain how you know this is my parents' cross. How did you know them? And why should I believe you even if you are telling the truth?"

"Twenty years ago, your father was the chief of this area. Things changes when you were born. You were supposed to be male, so when your mother gave birth to you, a girl, the tribe was appalled, especially Eric. He swore that he would never follow a female Alpha, so your parents hid you. One night though, when Eric thought you were with them he caused them to wreck their car, much of the same way Jessie did to you. When you weren't found in the car with your parents, Eric killed them to ensure he would be named Alpha. He took charge of the tribe and they have followed his orders ever since."

Kayla's eyes narrowed at the old markings on the cross that rose up from the snow. There was no doubt Kayla was torn. The weight of Matt's words crushed her as she reached out and touched the cold stone.

"How do you know this?" Kayla choked out, trying to keep her emotions under control.

"Because I was the one who hid you. I took you to the nearest town and branded you with my insignia, blended with your parents'." Matt touched Kayla's shoulder where her scar burned under his touch.

"That is why I don't follow your orders but why you can order the others to do your bidding. It is a combination of your Alpha blood and mine. Any it is also proof that you are the leader of this clan. You are their true Alpha and if you choose to stay, I would follow you as I followed your parents." Matt bowed lower than when he bowed to Eric, pledging his loyalty to Kayla.

Kayla shook her head and pressed her lips into a tight line. "No way. This isn't happening."

"That mark is the reason why you can keep your human form or shift whenever you want. It is why you can leave this place and never come back. But I implore you to stay. Take up your rightful place. Eric does not belong as Alpha. He is a poor ruler and a murderer."

Heat flashed through Kayla as she saw Eric's face in her mind. Eric's wrinkled brown skin and glaring eyes. If she had known about Eric before, she would have killed him then and there.

"The tribe won't follow me." Kayla finally said calming her anger. Matt pressed his lips into a tight smile.

"They will when you prove to them what you can do."

"But I have never shifted before. I don't even know how that works. Are you sure you have the right girl?"

"I have the right girl. And as far as shifting, you must train yourself to let go. I noticed your hand as you thought of Eric. Let that course through your body and take you over. You will be able to shift; you just haven't done it yet."

"But," Kayla began to protest because the thought of letting the animal out of its well-chained cage frightened her. She swallowed hard pushing the fear down.

"There are those who can help you. That means you will have to go back. I doubt Eric will let his son out of his sight anytime soon."

"Why would I want Jessie's help?"

"Jessie is not Eric's only son."

Kayla's eyebrows scrunched together as her heart split. "Nate."

Matt shook his head as Kayla tried to reel in the mountain of emotions crushing her. Matt raised his hand and placed it on Kayla's shoulder.

"Nate is not a bad kid. He is the outcast of that family. He will help you if you ask him. But you must make the choice to stand up to Eric."

Kayla stared out towards the freedom of the forest. For so long she had been alone, now suddenly she was offered the one thing she always wanted, a place to belong.

"My parents would have wanted me here. They would have wanted their daughter playing in these woods and the freedom to go." Kayla turned to Matt.

"Does Eric let the others leave?"

"No one can leave these parts. He keeps everyone away from others for fear of our secret getting out. But wolves are made to roam. Staying in one place makes us antsy, so to speak. I believe it is time for everyone to find their own way don't you?"

Kayla nodded as she pulled the pieces of herself together. "I think it's time to change things up."

"I was hoping you would say that."

Chapter 9

"Another barn? You have got to be joking." Kayla glanced about the rusty worn-down barn and shuddered. The thoughts of her previous encounter in a barn still haunted her; yet, here she was again. This barn was much smaller, with no post in the middle with chains. Only stacks of hay followed by several stalls for wild life. Besides the stench, Kayla found the place a little too busy for her comfort.

"I can't bring you back into town. Not yet anyway. Eric must think you have left for good. If he finds you, he will kill you. But, I won't let that happen. So be good and wait here. I will back by nightfall." Matt glared at Kayla with a stern glare. For a moment Kayla thought Matt could have been her dad. But the gray hairs peppering his hair and chin made Kayla giggle at the thought.

"Better yet, hide until I find you. If anyone else comes in here, they will try to kill you."

"But they won't be able to," Kayla snickered. Matt nodded and then scowled.

"Just stay out of sight, got it?"

"Fine." Kayla threw her hands up in surrender as Matt left her in the barn.

Kayla stroked the horse and fed the pigs, to pass the time. For the first time in forever, she was proud of her work. It seemed that domestication suited her. She didn't even mind messing with the pitch fork and tossing straw into the horse's stall for bedding. Sweat poured down her forehead, but she didn't mind. Hard labor felt good.

As the last of the sun's rays drifted into through the cracks of the wooden barn, Kayla heard footsteps stomping through the snow. She tossed the pitch fork into the pig's pen and scrambled for the horse's stall.

"You better not be messing with me old man."

Kayla's heart skipped a beat the moment she heard Nate's voice. She pulled herself up over the gate and dusted herself off waiting for him to come into the barn. The moments dragged on and Kayla began to wonder what was taking so long.

"I promise, she is the one he has been looking for all these years. How else could she get the others to stop and obey her demands?"

"Because maybe they are starting to see that Eric shouldn't be followed." Nate fired back and Kayla smiled. Maybe Matt was right about him after all. Maybe Nate would help her if only he would come into the barn.

"Of course this could be a ruse for you to get me busted by my dad. He is just begging for an excuse to toss me out of the tribe. If Kayla really is in there why doesn't she come out and say hi then."

The instant Kayla heard her name she raced for the barn doors. As she peeked through the crack, she noticed several men standing in the shrubs waiting for her to expose herself.

"Of course he sold me out," Kayla grumbled as she snuck back into the horse's stall waiting for the ambush.

Her heart pounded fiercely in her chest as she tried to think. There was only one way into the barn, but the door was wide enough for at least three men.

"What if they come in their wolf form?" Kayla wondered. How was she going to take them on if she couldn't shift? Kayla's eyes darted about the barn looking for the pitchfork she'd tossed earlier. At least that would be some kind of weapon that she could use to defend herself.

As Kayla plotted her defense, she didn't notice the creak in the barn doors, as they opened. The blood in her body ran cold and her hands began to tremble with fear.

"Concentrate," Kayla told herself as she waited for the attack.

"Kayla, Nate is here. Come out and speak with him."

Kayla remained silent as Matt called for her. Over the stench of manure, Kayla could smell Nate's musky scent. She could taste the salt of his skin on her tongue with each breath. But she remained still refusing to move.

"I know she is in here. I told her not to go anywhere," Matt said as he poked his head around in the stalls searching for her.

"Kayla?" Nate tried, and she held her tongue despite the longing that was tearing her apart.

"She bolted." Nate said giving up. "I knew she would. And you, old man, are going to go down in history as a deserter too, you know that?"

"Nate please, she is in here. I don't know why she is not coming out."

"Maybe because Nate is setting us both up." Kayla whispered hoping her voice would carry to their ears.

"Says who?" Nate lashed back as his eyes darted around the barn as Kayla's voice bounced off the walls.

"Those men in the bushes waiting for you to return. Or did you not notice them hunting and following you here? You're working for your dad." Kayla moved swiftly around the horse trying not to startle it as she crawled under the boards of the stall and into the next pen.

"I don't know what you are talking about." Nate defended himself again throwing his arms up into the air.

"Then look out the barn doors and see for yourself. There are three men waiting in bushes just beyond the shadows of the trees."

From where Kayla rested, she saw Nate and Matt walk over to the barn doors, turning their back on her. For a split second Kayla thought about making a run for it, but her senses kicked in negotiating with her instincts to remain still.

"I swear, I didn't know they followed me," Nate turned back around with his head and shoulders slumped.

"I can see why you don't trust me. This looks like I am about to sell you out."

"Matt, tell Nate to leave."

"But he can help you." Nate turned his head to stare at Matt with a confused expression on his face.

"Help with what?"

"Kayla has never shifted before. She needs someone to help her and seeing as how you two already have a connection, I thought that person should be you," Matt cleared his throat as he spoke the last words. Kayla could sense the awkwardness of coming from Matt, but Nate's expression was one Kayla was not expecting.

Nate's eyes widened as he scanned the barn searching for Kayla. Despite the fact she was covered in filth, she knew her cheeks were burning red.

"I would be honored to help you," Nate stated as he lifted his head up high. Something about Nate's stance made Kayla uneasy. It was as if Nate had just won a prize and that prize was Kayla. "I can show you how to shift, but then what?"

"Then I take out your dad." Kayla hissed as she glared at Nate wondering if he would step back knowing her intentions were not honorable.

"You mean to kill him?"

"Yes."

Nate dropped his head, contemplating, as Kayla and Matt waited for him to respond.

"It makes sense. I knew it would happen, eventually. I just didn't think I would have a part to play in it."

"You don't. All I need from you is to show me how to use my animal side. That's it. Nothing more, nothing less, so will you?"

Nate pressed his lips together and nodded.

"Good."

"But we can't do it here. There are too many eyes on this place. It will have to be someplace else. A place the others won't go." Nate rubbed his chin thinking of different safe places he could take Kayla to train her.

"The Old Mill Road is three miles away." Matt finally spoke. "Eric doesn't allow the others to go there. Says it is haunted or something to that effect."

"Superstitious old fool," Nate scoffed shaking his head. "Then that will be the place. Can you meet me there tomorrow at sunrise?"

"I'll be there."

"I will make sure, I won't be followed."

"You do that," Kayla grumbled as she watched Nate walk out of the barn leaving Matt alone with her.

The moment Matt closed the barn doors, Kayla crawled out from her hiding place.

"Do you think we can trust him not to rat us out?"

"I don't know," Matt shrugged as he pinched his nose. "Trust your feelings. But I think his loyalty is with you now."

"We will see come tomorrow," Kayla said as mud plopped down to the ground from her hair.

"You might want to clean up before you see him though."

"Hey, I had to improvise."

"I'll fetch you some clothes and you can stay here for the night. We can't risk the villagers seeing you and reporting back to Eric. Especially if they have eyes on this place."

"Oh goodie, another night in the barn."

"Would you rather sleep outside?" Matt crossed his arms over his chest and stared at Kayla. Kayla glanced around the open space and shrugged.

"Beggars can't be choosers now can they?"

Chapter 10

The sun's rays stretched out over the horizon causing the shadows of the trees to appear like fingers over the snowy ground. Kayla stood behind a tree taking in the view as the frozen landscape calmed her nerves. Her palms were sweaty and her heart raced. So much had happened in these past few days that she couldn't quite wrap her head around it all. The stillness that consumed her was pleasant and she breathed in deep, allowing the fresh air to fill her lungs.

"If you think this is nice, wait until you experience it as a wolf." The sound of Nate's voice pulled Kayla out of her meditation. She turned her head to see him walking towards her with his arms out.

"So how did you manage to get away from your babysitters?"

"I promise I didn't know they were following me."

Kayla scanned the surrounding area ensuring they were alone before she relaxed.

"How does this work?" Kayla asked turning her attention back towards the open forest. "Do I just close my eyes and think about it? Or should I envision myself that way?"

Nate laughed as he moved closer to Kayla. She cringed, the moment she felt his hands around her waist.

"You're seriously overthinking this. Changing into another form requires little concentration. In fact, you would do better if you let everything go."

"And how does one just 'let things go'?" Kayla twisted her head and glanced at Nate. He pulled her closer to him. The heat from his breath sent chills racing through Kayla's body. She shuddered as Nate held her.

"That feeling; that is the first step. Don't stop the shakes, let them consume you."

"What?" Kayla pulled away appalled at his words as if he just committed an unspeakable crime.

"Do you remember the other day in Alice's room? I saw your hands beginning to tremble, and you stopped it."

"I didn't want to hurt you or Alice."

"That sensation is the beginning of the shift. You have to let it pull you away from yourself and take you to another place."

"Maybe I should get Matt to help me with this."

Nate's laughter broke through the forest again, causing Kayla to grind her teeth. She didn't like the fact that Nate would be helping her. It felt as if she was somehow working with the enemy.

"Watch me." Nate stepped back from Kayla. With wide eyes, Kayla studied Nate as tremors ripped through his body morphing it into something else. The whole transformation took seconds, but with each passing moment, Kayla felt the urge to follow him.

Before Kayla could blink, a large russet-colored wolf with a white furry chest stood before her. Kayla stumbled back as she took in the size of the creature. Nate dropped to the ground and stared up at Kayla with his big gray eyes. Then, she watched as the wolf stood up on all fours and shivered. The hair fell from the creature's body like water and revealed a human Nate, once more.

"Okay." Kayla said with a wide-open mouth, too stunned for any other words. Nate stood tall with his shoulders back and a grin that stretched from ear to ear.

"Your turn. Clear your mind and just allow nature to take you over."

Kayla stood still and closed her eyes. With each breath she inhaled she forced herself to listen further and deeper into the forest. The birds in the trees and the scrapping of snake scales burrowing into the ground filled her ears. Even the soft rubbing of tree branches high in the canopy of the forest. Still, no change occurred.

"Stop. Stop. Stop. You're still overthinking this."

Kayla opened her eyes and huffed. With her hands in tight little balls, she allowed Nate to wrap his arms around her body.

"You are too tense. You have to relax. Think of something that is soothing. Something that will make you forget about everything."

"There is only one thing that will do that." Kayla mumbled, and sex was the furthest thing from her mind.

"I am not saying we act on anything. Just think about what turns you on and don't be afraid to let those emotions consume every part of your being."

Kayla closed her eyes again and allowed her mind to drift. She pushed aside who was holding onto her and simply allowed herself to feel the strong arms around her. She breathed in deeply taking in the musky scent of Nate behind her. Kayla imagined the twitch was Nate's cock begging for attention. Although it wasn't hard, she knew she could make it that way with a touch of her hand.

Kayla drifted into the fantasy playing out in her mind all the things she could do to him. She started with running her hand down his thigh and cupping his semi-erection. She would use her pinkie finger to play with the rim of his crown until it twitched and throbbed. Of course she wouldn't stop until she had Nate begging for more.

As the ideas swirled about her mind, she could feel the heat sparking within her. The flames licked every inch of her as it set her on fire. If she didn't act soon, she would be engulfed by the desire.

"That's it, don't stop," Nate cooed in her ear as moisture pooled in her panties. Her chest rose and fell in heavy pants as Nate's hand drifted over her body teasing her further into submission.

"Let it all go and don't hold anything back," his teeth grazed her earlobe as he spoke. The heat from his breath on her ear sent the flames higher until she twisted her body around and pushed Nate away from her.

He flew back with a wicked grin as she raced towards him. Without thinking, Kayla's form melted in the fire and a new form emerged out of the smoke. She glanced about as she found herself on four legs trembling.

"What the hell?" she said but her words came out as barks and whimpers. Nate smiled as he stood straight and walked over to her. The sensation of his hand running through the thick hair that now covered her body caused her to nip at his hand.

"Let's see what you can do." Nate stepped back and shifted. Kayla found herself staring at the large wolf again, kneeling before her, before he sprinted into the forest.

Instinct took over and Kayla found herself rushing towards Nate. With each stride, Kayla flew over the land. The cold air didn't bother her as she raced faster and faster overtaking Nate. She didn't realize how far she had gone until a howl, resonating through the forest, caused her to stop.

She dug her tough nails into the snow and skidded to a stop. Air pushed through her lungs faster and harder than ever before. With each breath new scents filled her nostrils. She could taste the meat from deer no more than a hundred yards away. She could feel the heat of a car's engine roaring down the highway despite her distance to the freeway. Kayla could see every snow flake that drifted from the top of the trees in perfect clarity.

"Pretty amazing isn't it?" Nate's voice boomed in her new ears as she whipped her head around to find him in human form. The heat from his body caused her to back away, it was far too intense for her to handle and her gut feeling told her to flee.

Nate approached slowly with his hands raised in the air. The soft tenderness of his gray eyes held her there like glue.

"Now shift back."

Kayla's head bobbed from side to side. There was too much for her to see and do in this form for her to shift back now. The wolf in her slowly began to overpower her will to do anything human.

"You have to shift back or let the wolf have you. Of course there are some that don't mind living a wolf's life, but you have things to do remember?"

As Nate spoke Kayla began pulling memories from her human life into the front of her mind. A cold chill started in her toes and began to extinguish the flames that consumed her. Kayla allowed the frosty air to push through her veins until the long fur coat vanished leaving her with her human self once more.

"Wow, that's impressive." Nate strolled over to Kayla and helped her back up to her feet. Kayla shivered as the last of the frost left her body.

"That was..." Kayla tried to find the right words, but it seemed like an outer body experience that could easily be passed off as a dream.

"It was real," Nate confirmed pointing to the tracks in the snow. "Congrats. Now let's do it again."

"Wait what?" Kayla's eyes grew wide as she thought about her wolf-self overpowering her again.

"You have to learn how to control it, if you want to take out Eric. He can shift on the fly with no hesitation. You need that kind of experience if you are going to surprise him."

"But I thought it was only at the new moon that he was allowed to change. Or any of you for that matter." Kayla's eyebrows scrunched together over the bridge of her nose, as she stared at Nate with a bewildered expression. Something about this wasn't adding up and Kayla could sense it in her bones.

"The new moon is just the time of the month we all shift together to show a united pack. Not everyone joins in. But you can bet that everyone in the village can shift whenever they want. They have had years of training. You, on the other hand, have never been allowed to let the wolf out. That is why its pull on you is so great. The more you do it, the more control you will gain. Now, do it again. Shift into your wolf and shift back into a human. You don't need to take off unless of course you are trying to run to Canada. But in that case, you may want to go that way." Nate pointed to his left and grinned the wicked little grin that Kayla was growing accustomed to.

She sucked in a deep breath and closed her eyes. As new fantasies played out in her mind, Kayla reached down between her legs to touch herself. There, she found her soft spot and let the passion ignite her once more. The moment her front feet touched the earth below her, she opened her eyes.

Nate leaned against a tree and for the first time, Kayla saw him as he was. Tall and slender with his shoulders arched back in a cocky stance. She marveled at his face. The way his lips parted as he spoke was hypnotizing. Never had Kayla seen a more stunning man. Sure, the men she had seen back home had strong builds. Their arms were like steel. But Nate's, his arms were thick and muscular. Kayla could see the grooves of his chest as he stood admiring her transformation.

There was no doubt he could snap her neck like a twig. But his eyes unlocked his softer nature. His gray eyes penetrated Kayla stealing the very breath she pulled in. Kayla shook her head trying to suppress the desire but the longer she remained in her wolf form the more she wanted him.

"Long enough. Change back." Nate pushed himself off the tree and waited with his arms crossed. Kayla tried to find the frost to extinguish the flames once again, but her mind was stuck on one thing.

"Kayla?" Nate drew closer and Kayla could smell the saltiness of his skin. She wanted to take him right then and there.

"Eric." That was the trigger. Kayla glanced over her shoulder and raced back towards the village. She knew if she was going to take him out, now would be the time.

Before Kayla reached the small barn on Matt's property, Nate was there to intercept her. He shoved his massive body into hers driving her back towards the safety of the woods. Kayla nipped at him as he drove her back. Between the snarls and the desire, Kayla started slipping more into the wolf than she did before.

Nate sank his fangs into her hind leg. Pain shot through her causing her to stop. Without warning, the frost stung her toes and before she could get the flames back, her fur coat was gone and she was human once again.

Kayla panted on the cold ground confused as to how she had gotten so close to Matt's. Then the images of racing came back to her, and she shuddered to think of what she might have done to Nate. Carefully she pulled herself up to her feet and looked around. Nate remained hidden in the shadows.

She moved closer with her hands up. "I am so sorry."

"It was my fault. I thought the name would trigger your human side, but it back fired."

Kayla moved over to Nate and cupped her hands around his head. "I didn't mean to hurt you."

Before Nate could protest, Kayla pegged him between her body and the tree. Nate's tongue parted her lips and swirled around her mouth as they embraced. In one swoop, Nate spun Kayla around causing the bark of the tree to claw Kayla's back. He pulled back to nibble the length of Kayla's neck until her reach her earlobe.

"I will not be gentle," he whispered. His hot breath on her ear caused her body to tremble. Kayla didn't know what she should do. A part of her wanted to embrace him and pull him to her, but her head screamed at her to shift. Conflicted by the emotions and thoughts, Kayla concentrated, refusing to let the wolf regain its hold on her.

Nate's hand brushed her cheek coaxing her. "Look at me," he said as his lips kissed against Kayla's jawline and back down her neck.

Kayla peeked through her eyelids. His eyes were burning with desire as he took a step back. The gap between them was like a gorge, but Nate's gaze locked her in place.

"I want you, Kayla. I want all of you. The girl and the wolf."

Kayla stared at his unflinching eyes as her nipples grew hard from the icy air that licked them. She pressed her body closer to his, closing the gap as her leg lifted up to encircle his hips. The cool breeze played with the tips of Kayla's hair which tickled her back sending chills coursing through her.

"Turn around," Nate groaned as Kayla unlocked her lips from his mouth.

"Kayla," her name rolled off his tongue so smoothly. He lured her in with tenderness. Kayla turned around slowly to catch a glimpse of Nate's hard cock eagerly waiting for her. Nate stood like a statue in a garden with his chiseled physique. Kayla dropped to her knees and stuck her ass in the air.

His hands groped at Kayla's breast as he pushed his hips into hers. His hard cock nudged the crack of Kayla's ass as he pinched her nipples. With his free hand, Nate wrapped his fingers around his cock and eased it closer to her wet pussy.

Kayla reached between her legs and grabbed the bottom of his shaft to force Nate's cock into her. She had been teasing herself for so long that this moment was all she wanted. As Nate entered her, the tremors began wreaking havoc on her body. She tried to ease them, but the harder Nate pushed into her, the more she wanted to shift.

"You can't hurt me," Nate reminded her as his hands clamped down around her waist keeping her pinned to him. Kayla groaned as he filled her up. With each thrust of his hips, his cock fed the desire. Kayla's eyes rolled back as she let herself enjoy Nate as much as humanly possible.

Nate pulled back just enough to keep Kayla open before driving into her again. Again Kayla cried out as Nate entwined his fingers into Kayla's hair and drove into her with more intensity than ever before.

"You were holding back on me before." Kayla huffed as Nate twisted her hair in his grip.

"I had to," he panted.

"And now?"

"I told you, I want you every way you will allow me."

Chapter 11

Kayla pushed her body against Nate's taking his shaft deep into her. Every thrust caused her body to tremble. Each time the shakes occurred, Nate pulled out causing the chilling effect that calmed Kayla down.

"Is this how it will always be?" Kayla asked as Nate held his position with only the crown of his cock buried in her body.

"Until you gain more experience, then we can have some real fun."

"Why not now?"

"I'm afraid that if we tried, you may not come back to me."

Nate drove his shaft into her body filling her up once more. Kayla cried out in pleasure as her juices flowed out of her, covering Nate's thick cock. Kayla glanced up to the sky. In the blackness of space, Kayla saw her life laid out before her. She could see Nate by her side and the emptiness she carried with her all these years had gone. With every push, Nate melted into Kayla and she wanted nothing more than to please him. As the soft pale blues of night shifted to dark purple before fading to black Kayla made up her mind. No matter what the future held, she would have Nate in it one way or another.

The more Nate throbbed in her, the more she wanted him. It was a constant game of give and take until Nate could no longer handle Kayla's unquenchable lust.

"I'm..." Nate panted as he jerked his body away from Kayla. Kayla scrambled to Nate's cock with her mouth open wide to receive his hot cum. Nate stroked his shaft jerking faster and squeezing the base of it tightly until the white goo left the tip and sprayed out.

The moment Nate released his seed, he dropped to his knees. "Damn, woman. How long can you go?"

Kayla giggled as she licked the tip of his red head tasting the salty fluid that remained. "A while."

Nate dropped down to rest as Kayla snuggled next to him. Nate wrapped his arm around Kayla as they stared up into the diamond filled sky.

"Still want Matt to show you how?" Nate chuckled. Kayla dove her head into his chest stifling her laugh.

"Did he know this would happen?"

"It kind of happens with all the new shifters. That is why there are no rules here when it comes to this. If you are invited, you can play."

Alice drifted into Kayla's mind as she recalled Jessie's stern gaze finding Alice with them in the bedroom.

"Is Alice with Jessie then?"

Nate pressed his lips together and nodded.

"Oh." Kayla kept her eyes glued to the sky above them as Nate regained a normal breathing rhythm.

"Are you really going to kill my dad?"

Kayla propped herself up on her elbow and stared at Nate. She sucked in a deep breath and steadied herself. "Yes."

"I knew that," Nate mumbled. "I was just hoping there might be another way."

"He killed my parents."

Nate rose up to meet Kayla's eyes. The shock Kayla found was unexpected.

"What?" he asked.

"Matt showed me their cross. He said that my parents were the tribe's leaders and that your father killed them once they couldn't produce a male heir."

"That's not how things work. My dad would never harm anyone."

"Really? Then why doesn't he allow the villagers to leave? Don't you think that is kinda of imprisoning them?"

"Did Matt tell you that too?"

Kayla nodded as she stared at Nate. The passion flickered out as Nate studied Kayla.

"If anyone wants the title of the tribe leader it's Matt. He has been an outcast since the beginning. Why do you think he lives on the edge of the village?"

"But.."

Kayla paused as Nate rose. She watched as he dusted the leaves off his body and shook out his hair.

"There are some things that my dad has done in his past, but murder is not one of them."

"Nate?"

"I had hoped that maybe helping you would show you the light, but clearly you only want to follow blindly." Nate turned his back on Kayla as his shoulders dropped.

"Find a new teacher to help you shift if you are on this suicide mission. I won't help you anymore."

"But Nate."

"No, Kayla."

Her mouth dropped as Nate shifted into his wolf form and bolted into the darkness.

Kayla rose slowly wondering what just happened. For a brief moment she pictured her whole life. Everything down to where she would live. Nate was the answer to every question she ever wanted or needed to know. But now, he was gone and she didn't know if he would ever come back.

As she strolled through the crisp night air back to Matt's place, Kayla pondered over Nate's words. Perhaps she was blindly following Matt. But he had helped her from the start. He had given her a place to stay when all the others had turned her away. Matt had told her about her parents and their untimely demise. Nothing that Nate said made any sense to her.

"But how well do you know Matt?" Kayla's inner voice asked as she approached the small barn on Matt's property. The soft glow of lights glowed in the barn as Kayla walked towards it. With each step, a sinister pang stabbed her chest. Kayla knew it had something to do with Nate and she couldn't bear to think about it anymore. He was gone and once again, she was alone in the world.

Kayla pushed through the barn doors to find a pile of neatly folded clothes waiting for her. The idea of walking around in the nude had never bothered her before, but somehow seeing the clothes made her hyper aware of her body. She threw them on without thinking and sat down on the pile of straws.

"Eric found out your parents had a girl and would never serve a woman." Matt's words played back in her mind as she thought about Nate. The spark in Matt's eyes as he tied her to the barn flashed before her eyes. Even the twisted smirk on Matt's face when she had no power over him played back in her mind.

Kayla rubbed the scar on her shoulder as she contemplated her next move. Maybe there was something to Nate's indecision about killing his dad. Maybe Eric was nothing more than an overprotective father wanting to keep the village secret from the outside world.

Kayla rose and scanned the barn. The only way she would ever get any answers was by asking. Kayla bobbed her head determined to find them and stormed out of the barn.

"First stop," Kayla glanced over at the small hut that was Matt's home and walked up to the front door. With a hard rap of her knuckles, Kayla waited for an answer.

Chapter 12

"Kayla, back so soon?" Matt smiled wide as he opened the screen door allowing Kayla into his home. Kayla forced herself to smile through the doubt that was wreaking havoc on her mind.

Matt's house was smaller than Alice's was, but she could tell by the same carpet and layout, that it was similar. Kayla walked through the door and found the living room easily enough. She plopped down on the hard leather sofa and stared at the dirt between her fingernails.

The sound of the screen door shutting threw Kayla off. For a moment the metal sounded like a latch but there were other things for her to concentrate on. Matt walked in and took the soft La-Z-Boy recliner in front of the fire. Kayla could feel his glare burning her as they sat in silence.

"Well?" Matt finally asked. "How did it go?"

"I couldn't do it." Kayla lied. She glanced up to find Matt leaning back in his chair. His eyes flickered with the light from the fire. Kayla flinched as Matt pulled himself up and leaned over. He extended his hand out and rubbed her knee.

"It's okay you know. Sometimes, you just need the right person to show you how. I thought Nate would be a good fit to unleash that animal, but there are others."

"I don't think anyone can help me. Maybe there is something wrong with me. Maybe I am just too old to have it unleashed. Nate said that those in the village learned early and that maybe since I didn't grow up with it, it won't come out."

"Nonsense. Your parents had it, which means you have it." Matt's hand rubbed faster as he spoke causing Kayla to jerk her leg away. Matt pulled back his hand and smiled.

"The best thing for you to do is try again tomorrow."

"Nate said I am hopeless and to find someone new."

"Did he now?" Matt stood and walked over to the kitchen. "Did he say why other than he thinks you're helpless?"

"He asked if I was really going to kill his dad."

"And what did you say?" A new aroma filled the air as Matt spoke. Kayla tried not to turn around and remained focused on the fire and the pictures that littered the mantle.

One in particular flickered with an orange glow from the fire.

Kayla rose to her feet and moved over to the picture. A couple carrying a young child smiled back at her. The dark-haired woman looked tired. Kayla couldn't help but feel a stab of regret as she stared back at the new family.

"Well?" Matt asked. His voice startled her as he stood beside her with a cup of tea in his hand. Matt extended the cup to Kayla. She breathed in deep, taking in the gentle aroma of lavender and mint before accepting it from him.

"I told him yes. That he killed my parents, and that Eric has to pay."

"Mmm." Matt's eyes tightened as he sipped on the cup in his hand before moving over to the La-Z-Boy and sat down.

"That may be why he doesn't want to help. I thought he would want someone new in charge."

Matt kept his eyes locked on Kayla as she sat the picture back down on the mantle and studied the other images. Each one was of a different place and time. Memories that Matt clearly didn't want to forget.

"Maybe I can find a way on my own," Kayla said as she set the cup down on the mantle.

"Don't put that there," Matt barked. Kayla removed the cup quickly and glanced over to Matt. He huffed and exhaled until his nerves were calm again.

"That mantle has a lot of memories for me, ones that I wouldn't want ruined by a cup of split tea."

"I get it, sorry." Kayla set the mug down on the coffee table and took her place on the stiff leather couch again.

"Look, I didn't mean to come here to disrupt your night. I just thought you would like to know how it went today."

"Well, thank you." Matt grinned. Kayla nodded her head before she pushed off the sofa and made her way back to the door.

"Kayla?"

Matt's voice lingered on the air sending chills racing through Kayla's body. She paused with her hand on the doorknob.

"What's up?" she tried to appear more relaxed than she was.

"If you weren't able to shift today, then why are you in the clothes I set out for you?"

Kayla's blood ran cold. She hadn't thought the clothes were a test. She glanced over her shoulder and smiled. "The others are in the barn dirty. I just didn't want to go to bed like that, you know."

Matt nodded. Kayla tried the knob. The instant Matt heard the jiggle of the metal he jumped from his seat. Kayla twisted her body around to find him shifting into his wolf form. With no time to spare, she jumped out of the way as Matt crashed through his front door. The sound that came out of Kayla startled her as she tried to scramble over the wolf and run for the woods. At least the darkness could mask her.

With each stride she took, she tried to force the wolf out of her. But, fear stole her courage as she jumped and hurdled over fallen trees trying to get to the village.

"Come on Kayla." She screamed at herself. "Shift already."

Matt tore through the shrubs after her, nipping at her heels. Every time she weaved, Matt was right there to counter. Her only hope was to climb. In the darkness Kayla pushed her human legs to go faster. If she couldn't make it to the village, she would at least get to the highway.

In the dead of night, howls ripped through the area. The echo of the tribe caused Matt to pause. The moment was long enough for Kayla to reach a tree branch and hoist herself up into the air. With one final heave, she pulled herself up and continued to climb. The sound of the wolves grew closer as Matt jumped and nipped at the branches.

"Go away. Leave me alone." Kayla screamed as the last branch she tried snapped under her weight causing her to tumble down. She hit the ground hard, knocking the air out of her lungs. Matt was on her. His snout pressed against her forehead as drool dripped from his sharp teeth.

Kayla closed her eyes waiting for the bite. The crashing of branches and the thud of bodies slamming into one other pulled her eyes open.

"Nate?"

The russet wolf sank his teeth into the white-gray wolf that was Matt. A long howl ripped through the air causing Kayla to cover her ears as the two fought to the death.

"Stop, Nate he'll kill you!"

Nate didn't stop. He was faster than Matt and had more reason to fight than ever before. Nate thrashed at Matt with his claws digging into the white wolf's fur coat. Again Matt let out a cry as blood dripped from an open wound. Kayla scrambled to her feet trying to find something that could help Nate. It was in that moment that the heat filled her.

Fire engulfed every inch of her body and she found herself on four legs charging at Matt. The white wolf was outnumbered. Kayla lunged at Matt, as Nate distracted him long enough to give Kayla the shot she needed. Kayla let the wolf take over and she went in for the kill.

With her jaw clamped around Matt's neck, Kayla chomped down, ending Matt then and there. Nate pulled back and shifted as Kayla continued to thrash the white wolf around the forest slamming him into the trees, as she ran with him.

"Kayla!" Nate cried out for her but she had disappeared into the forest.

Chapter 13

Kayla dragged Matt across the highway and plopped him down beside the white cross. Seeing her parents marked grave gave her the frost she needed to shift back. She sucked in a deep breath and let the fur coat drop off her.

"Kayla?" Nate's voice was far away, but still Kayla turned her head towards the direction from which it came. In the dark shadows she saw Nate streaking through the woods towards her.

"You came back." Kayla gasped as she saw the blood on Nate's arm.

"I couldn't leave you with him after I found out the truth."

"And what was that?"

Nate crossed the highway and stood with Kayla beside the broken white wolf.

"My father told me what happened, and he wants you to come back so you can hear the real story."

"You mean so I can hear more lies."

"No lies."

"Is that the only reason why you came for me?" Kayla gazed up at Nate hoping against hope that maybe the life she envisioned could come to be. Nate grabbed Kayla by the hand and pulled her to him.

"I told you I wanted all of you; both the wolf and the girl. I meant what I said. We are connected now in ways that you don't understand, but I can help you. I can show you a new world if you will let me."

"I want all of that." Kayla said as she pulled Nate to her and embraced him.

Their lips crashed against each other and Kayla's body trembled with delight. After all this time she had finally found a home and a place where she belonged. Nate pulled away and hugged her.

"There is so much for you to learn." Nate cupped his hand around Kayla's face and smiled at her. "But first, you should get cleaned up."

"I probably look like a monster don't I?"

"Kind of, yeah."

Kayla let Nate's hand drop to his side as she moved around the white wolf and the cross.

"Don't you want a souvenir?" Nate asked dropping to Matt's side. Kayla watched as Nate lifted Matt's head.

"No. Leave him. I don't want to think about him or what he did ever again."

Kayla glared at Nate as Nate dropped the white wolf's head and stood up. "Why did you think I would want something like that?"

"Some keep tokens of their kills. Matt's is his mantle."

"Those pictures? Are they? Were they?" Nate nodded with a sober expression as he took Kayla's hand.

"That family in one of the pictures. Did Matt really kill the whole family?"

"Not the whole family. The girl in the picture killed him."

Epilogue

Kayla stood on the front porch of her new house staring at the ruby-red colors filling the sky. The warmth of the sun heated her skin as she watched the sun rise above the horizon, casting long shadows of the trees that lined her new place. The birds in the trees whistled and squawked as they rose for the day. She sucked in a deep breath as Nate's arms wrapped around her waist.

"Not bad, huh?" He asked kissing her neck as he pressed his body closer to hers. Kayla rubbed his arms as she squeezed him tighter.

"A girl could get used to this."

"Are you going to be ready in an hour?"

"No." Kayla grimaced as she thought about what the day held for her. Despite the fact that Eric was no longer opposed to her staying, she knew that Nate's dad wasn't too thrilled about her dating his son. Today was his sixtieth birthday. The whole village had been preparing for weeks.

"It will be fine, I promise you. You are one of us now."

"How far did you say Canada was again?"

"Don't be silly. You won't want to miss this event."

"But your dad doesn't even like me."

"Today is for him. But tonight is for the tribe. Trust me. You will want to be here for this."

Kayla shrugged Nate off her and turned around in his arms. She pressed her lips against his and entwined her fingers into his hair.

"You can't distract me with sex all the time." Nate mumbled as Kayla parted his lips with her tongue. She rubbed her breast against his, hoping Nate would feel her hard nipples under her cotton shirt. Nate hungrily kissed her back wrapping his fingers around her butt cheeks before pulling away.

"Nice try, but we can do that later. Right now, you need to get ready."

Kayla sighed as she released Nate and strolled through the door and up the stairs. Once she reached her bedroom door, she pushed it open.

"Of all the days," she sighed as she headed to the closet. She pulled open the closet doors, before jumping back. The blood in her veins froze as her mother stared at her from the closet mirror.

"Mom?" Kayla's mother reached out for her with her mouth agape trying to speak to her. Kayla blinked and the image vanished.

"Kayla?" Nate called to her anxiously and he flew up the stairs when Kayla didn't respond. Kayla's eyes remained locked on the mirror as Nate dropped to the floor beside her.

"Kayla? What's wrong?"

"I think I saw my mother in the mirror."

Kayla's throat was hoarse and dry. Her tongue scrapped the roof of her mouth as she spoke. Nate rubbed Kayla's leg, trying to get her to look at him.

"Kayla, I told you, you still have a lot to learn about being a wolf."

END

Origins of the Alpha
The Wolf Pack Bloodlines Series

Amelia Wilson

Table of Contents:

Prologue

Chapter 1

Chapter 2

Chapter 3

Chapter 4

Chapter 5

Chapter 6

Chapter 7

Chapter 8

Chapter 9

Chapter 10

Chapter 11

Chapter 12

Chapter 13

Epilogue

Prologue

History, they say, is written by the victors. Those that have conquered their enemies have the power to rewrite tales as they see fit. Those tales soon become legends. However, there are three sides to every story. The truth is often lost in translation. Only the dead know the truth and only they hold the secret of how man was cursed to become animal.

Chapter 1

"Will you stop?"

Kayla's giggles filled the corner of the tiny diner. The vinyl cushion squeaked under Nate's weight as he inched closer to her. Kayla scooted away, refusing to give into his carnal desires. With quick reflexes, Nate wrapped his arm around her shoulders keeping her in place as he forced her to sit next to him.

"Where do you think you are going? You know I want you close," he said as he slipped his free hand under the table. His hand was hot and soothing on her knee. Just his touch caused her body to react in unexpected ways. For a moment Kayla wanted nothing more than to let him do as he wished. She cupped her hand on his and moved his hand up her leg until his fingers grazed the hem of her dress. Her eyes scanned the small diner.

She wondered how many people would know what they were up to. From the corner of her eye, she spotted several people stealing glances at them, as Nate's little finger crawled up her thigh. She sucked in a deep shallow breath as the tip of his finger reached the thin cotton of her panties.

She let Nate have his fun, even under the disapproving glares. Her heart raced as he pushed aside the elastic and moved his finger over her lips. Kayla gripped the table waiting for his finger to penetrate her.

"You are such a tease," she scolded as Nate laughed and pulled his hand away.

"That's just a little something to get you going for tonight." Kayla grunted as Nate laughed. The other people in the diner quickly turned away the moment she met their gaze. Although Kayla had been in the village for over a month now, she could still feel an uneasy vibe that sent chills through her.

Of course a few accepted her: Alice, Adam, and of course Nate. However, the others: Jessie, Eric, and the rest of the tribe, found her presences disturbing. Kayla couldn't quite put her finger on it and wondered if she would ever be accepted.

"What's wrong?" Nate whispered as he leaned in closer. Kayla shivered as his fingers drifted over her neck as he spoke.

"They are staring at me again."

"Never mind them. They will come around eventually."

"But..." Kayla began to protest but Nate pressed his lips on hers, silencing her doubt. Her eyes drifted over the diner as Nate parted her lips with his tongue. Kayla noticed Jessie staring at them from the center of the diner. His hands were holding a burger, ready to chop down on it, but he had frozen in mid-air. Kayla quickly pulled back and shoved Nate away from her.

"Maybe I should just go home," Kayla mumbled as she sat up straight.

"You know, if you lived with me, we could go home together."

Kayla's eyes popped open as she stared at Nate with bewilderment. "Don't joke about that."

"I wasn't joking. I am being serious. You could live with me and we could be together."

"Nate, I..." Kayla dropped her gaze as she struggled to find the right words to use without breaking his heart.

"I know what you are going to say, but it's not too soon." Nate's hand slipped from her shoulders and cupped her face. Kayla couldn't bring herself to look at him.

"How many times now have you complained about living with Alice? If you live with me, then all your stuff would be at my place and you wouldn't have to go sneaking back home to get more clothes."

"It's not that I don't want to. It's just..." Kayla sighed as she spoke, fighting with herself as she tried not to look at Nate. She couldn't stand hurting him. Not after all he has done for her.

"What then?" he dropped his hand and stared at her with wide eyes.

"I haven't really had a roommate since I lived with my parents. I don't consider Alice a roommate, either, because neither one of us is ever home. We are more like ships passing in the night and it works."

"So, you don't want to come home with me, tonight?"

"I didn't say I wouldn't come over. I just don't think moving in would be a good idea."

"But half of your wardrobe is already at my place."

"How about we just focus on tonight," Kayla smiled as her hand slipped under the table and raced up Nate's leg. With her eyes sparkling in the soft candlelight, Kayla knew she had him right where she wanted him.

"How is it that you use sex to get out of everything?" Nate huffed as Kayla traced the hem of his zipper with her finger.

"It's a gift."

"Well it won't work, not this time." Nate sat back and crossed his arms. Kayla laughed as her fingers pressed harder into his jeans, tracing this manhood and feeling it twitch under the fabric. She wondered how long she would have to play with him until he caved. The game was on and Kayla wasn't taking any prisoners, at least not tonight.

"Really?" Kayla's lips pulled up at the corners as she scooted closer to him and cupped her hand over his crotch. Nate sucked in a deep breath as he felt her hand clamped around him. The heat from Kayla's hand scorched him and he couldn't deny his wants. His cock twitched under her touch. Kayla giggled as she pulled her hand away, raking her nails ever so lightly over his inner thigh.

"You are driving me crazy you know that?"

"Well, you started it. I am just making sure you know who is going to end it." Kayla leaned in closer making sure her breasts rubbed against his arm as she spoke. Nate inhaled as he stared at her.

"I want you now."

"Then take me, right here."

Nate's eyes shifted about the diner. Kayla could see the wheels in his head turning as he contemplated the idea.

"You want to pull me out of this booth, throw my body over the table and fuck me right here don't you?" Her fingers traced his cock as she painted the picture for him with every detail in perfect clarity.

"Do it. Take me right here. Lift up my dress, push my panties to the side and push your hard thick cock deep inside me. Fill me up as all these people watch you do it." Kayla's breath tickled Nate as the urge to do as she wanted grew. They both knew all she had to do was command him, and he would have no choice.

With sweaty palms, Nate's eyes closed as Kayla's fingers pinched his crown between her fingers. "The only thing stopping you is two thin layers of clothing."

"And the fact that we could get arrested."

"They would probably join in," Kayla hissed as she continued to play.

"Will you two get a room already?"

Kayla snapped her head up. There, standing at the edge of their table with a wide grin was Alice. The look in her eyes was accusing and Kayla swiftly moved her hand away from Nate.

"Hello Alice," Nate straightened himself in the booth.

"So will you be there tomorrow? I have to take a head count so I know how much food to make."

"Make for what?" Kayla asked. She glanced at Nate, wondering what Alice was talking about. Something about the drop in Nate's voice tugged at Kayla, suggesting he was hiding something from her.

"Yes, we'll be there."

"Be where? What is going on?" Kayla glanced between Nate and Alice hoping one of them would let her in on the secret.

"A party," Alice nearly skipped as she spoke. Clearly the excitement and suspense was killing her.

"Poor Alice," Kayla thought as she watched the girl nearly jumping out of her skin. "That girl will never be able to keep any secrets."

"Oh." Kayla's eyes lingered on Nate hoping he would give away some information. Nate pressed his lips together and drooped his eyes suddenly, all too interested in the empty plate before him.

"It's Eric's birthday party. Everyone will be there." Alice spilled the secret in a rush, her face beaming with joy.

"Well, I won't be going then." Kayla shifted her weight and pulled back from Nate. The last thing she wanted to do was spend time with a man who hated her. She could feel her skin crawl as she entertained the thought for a split second, before shoving and kicking the idea out of her mind.

"Come on, it will be fun." Alice stopped bouncing and glared at Kayla.

"That man hates me. The last thing I want to do is go to his party. Besides, I doubt he even wants me there."

"He wants you there," Nate chimed in. "He wouldn't want the village to think that he had excluded anyone."

"Nate's right you know. Eric wants EVERYONE there," Alice added. "It's going to be huge. Please tell me you will be there."

"If everyone is going, then I doubt I will be missed."

"Come on Kayla, birthdays are a big thing around here. I promise it'll be fun. You'll see." Alice's eyes grew big as she batted her lashes. Her bottom lip puffed out as she begged. Kayla couldn't help but laugh as Alice's pout grew.

"What are you, five?" Kayla chuckled as Alice turned up the puppy-dog eyes.

Despite the nagging in her gut, Kayla sighed. "Fine," she huffed. "I'll come. But I won't like it."

"You sure are being difficult tonight, you know that?" Nate glanced at Kayla with a half grin. Alice jumped up and down clapping her hands at the victory.

"It starts at nine."

"At night? I thought Eric went to bed at like seven o'clock."

"No, nine in the morning, Silly. But the major stuff won't happen till after twelve."

"The party is ALL day?" Kayla's eyes bulged. The thought of spending all day with Eric repulsed her.

"I told you this was going to be big. Eric's parties are the biggest event of the year," Alice beamed. "So I will see you there. Don't be late or call me saying you'll be sick. You are going and that's final."

"Fine," Kayla raised her hands in the air in surrender.

"Good," Alice flashed another brilliant smile before rushing off to the next table to spread the good news about the party to others.

"Wow," Nate smirked as he grabbed the check fold and glanced inside.

"What?" Kayla wondered and instinctively reached for her small purse at her side. "Need cash?"

"No. Not that, it's just that you are being so stubborn tonight."

"I am not being stubborn."

Nate chuckled as he grabbed the bill and then cocked his head. Kayla's eyes drifted to his lips as they curled up as he fought back his laughter.

"First you don't want to move in, and then you don't want to go to a party. Next you are going to say that you are too tired to come home with me tonight."

"You could always change my mind about the third thing," Kayla's mind shifted back to all the things she wanted to do to Nate. The idea of just the two of them in a dark room somewhere made her tingle.

"Good, because I have other plans for us tonight, if you aren't too tired," Nate whispered as his lips brushed Kayla's ear. She giggled as Nate's tickling breath caused her body to shiver. Nate slipped away from Kayla and pulled himself out of the booth.

"Do you now?" Kayla scooted to the edge of the booth and reached out for Nate's extended hand. As she stood, all eyes shifted to her. In the back of her mind, she knew the other patrons of the diner were listening to her. She just couldn't understand why her life impacted theirs so much.

As Kayla and Nate paid for their meals at the cash register, Kayla couldn't help but scan the diner once more. The moment her eyes landed on anyone, they quickly dropped their gaze. Kayla squeezed Nate's hand and sucked in a deep breath.

"You okay?" Nate asked as he slipped his wallet into his back pocket. Kayla nodded and followed him out of the diner and into the night. The moment the warm air night air swirled around her, Kayla exhaled.

"You sure you are okay?"

"It's just strange for me."

"What's that?" Nate smiled and curled Kayla's arm around his as they strolled down the street.

"This is still really strange for me you know," Kayla admitted. "I don't think I will get used to the idea of staying in one place."

"Well, if you run, I run." Nate said with a smile as he stopped suddenly. Kayla hadn't noticed and stumbled into Nate's awaiting arms. Under the light of the moon, Nate caressed Kayla.

"Do you think they will ever accept me here?" Kayla asked Nate, as they began walking again.

"Are you kidding? Alice loves you."

"But your father and brother have issues."

"Yeah, but those are their problems, not yours. You just keep being you and they will come to love you, as I do." Kayla paused and stared at Nate with wide eyes.

"Did you say you love me?"

"I thought that was pretty obvious by now. I mean I have been trying to get you to move in with me since the day we met, so yeah."

"But love?" Kayla smeared the word love as if it was a vile evil thing, to be avoided at all costs. She did care for Nate, after all, he helped her with Matt and she had a connection with him like no one else, but love? Was that the right word for it?

"Yes. Love. Deal with it." Nate said as he stopped at the passenger's side of his jeep and unlocked the door. Kayla stole one more glance at the small town around her. The light of the moon danced on the glass windows.

"You coming?" Nate asked waiting by the open door. Kayla climbed in and settled into the seat. Nate climbed in on the other side and slipped his keys into the ignition. The low rumble of the engine soothed Kayla. It didn't take long for the small village to disappear behind the veil of night.

They sat side by side in silence, as Nate drove down the road. With each bend, Kayla's nervousness grew. She envisioned a life with Nate and could see it so clearly in her mind. But still, a twist in her gut refused to let her see it through.

"Here we are," Nate said with a smile as he pulled down the gravel road to his place. The small house in the field was beginning to feel like home to her. She flashed a smile at him as he pulled up to the house and cut the engine. She climbed out of the jeep and waited for Nate. Together they walked up the three steps hand-in-hand and paused at the closed door.

"You seem off tonight," Nate stated as he slipped the key into the lock.

"I'm fine, promise." Kayla lifted her head to stare at Nate. She pushed the doubts and fears from her as Nate pulled open the door. The darkness of the little two-bedroom house was chilling. Although Kayla could see every detail, the shadows intimidated her. She stepped in and set her keys down on the small table. Abruptly Nate lifted her off her feet.

"Hey," Kayla protested as Nate whisked her to the bedroom.

"I told you," he said as his lips crashed into her neck. "I have plans for us tonight."

Kayla closed her eyes as Nate's fingers tugged at the hem of her dress hiking it up to her hips. The air flowed around her sending chills through her as Nate's hot breath drifted down her body until he was on his knees.

"What are you doing?" She asked peeking down to find Nate pulling her thin cotton panties down with his teeth.

"Nothing," he smirked as he pushed the fabric of her dress up higher and his head disappeared under the fabric of her dress.

She laughed as he struggled to get her undies off her. Only when he pulled back in frustration, did she slip her hands under her dress. The tight elastic of her panties snapped as she slipped her fingers under the elastic and shimmied them down. With her thin panties at her ankles,

Nate released her dress and lifted Kayla's feet up one at a time.

"Better?"

"Much." Nate huffed as he pulled the dress back up to her hips. Kayla waited for Nate with her arms up in the air for him to slip the fabric over her head. She leaned in pressing her lips against his and Nate ripped the dress away from Kayla and tossed it to the floor.

"Nice," Kayla mumbled between kisses.

"I think so," Nate smiled as his arms wrapped around her waist and threw her back onto the bed. Kayla hit the soft pillows and giggled as Nate moved to the edge of the bed and began licking her inner thigh. She sucked in a deep breath as scooted up towards the pillows.

"Where do you think you are going?" Nate grumbled as Kayla slipped through his grasp.

A smile played at the corner of her lips as Nate crawled over the bed. He remained crouched like a tiger in the jungle, hunting its prey, as he moved. Kayla bit her lower lip watching him. Her body craved his and she couldn't deny the urgency of taking him. But, still she waited.

"Not fair," Kayla giggled as Nate sat up to pull his cotton shirt up over his head. The moment Nate's head was shrouded, Kayla jumped up. She wrapped her arms around his neck keeping him locked with his hands above his head. With one hand, Kayla held the fabric of his shirt and began nibbling on the tender spot of his neck. The salty taste of his skin filled her mouth as her tongue drifted over his chiseled shoulders.

"You want me?" Kayla whispered as she played with his jeans with her free hand.

"Yes." Nate groaned. Kayla's eyes drifted towards Nate's zipper to find it bulging from his erection. For a split second Kayla thought about leaving him with his little problem. Then the idea slipped out of her mind and Nate wiggled from his restraints, pulling his shirt off at the same time.

"Your turn," Nate said as his hands flew to the buttons on Kayla's shirt.

"There is an easier way," Kayla laughed as she watched Nate struggle with the small plastic buttons. In one fail swoop, Kayla pulled at the hem of her shirt. Buttons flew across the room as Kayla exposed herself to Nate. In the darkness, their hunger grew.

Chapter 2

Kayla leaned down and curled her tongue around Nate's nipple. The warm hot breath against his skin made his body tremble under Kayla's hands. Her tender lips caressed his body as her hand flowed over his smooth chest before dropping to his hips.

"I think we have a problem," Kayla mumbled as her fingers inched down into Nate's jeans.

"Then maybe we should do something about that don't you think?" Nate huffed as Kayla nibbled down his body until she reached the hem of his pants. With Kayla's beautiful wide eyes staring up at him Nate smiled and wrapped his fingers into her hair, forcing her to go further.

Kayla tugged at the button of his jeans as her fingers played with the bulge in his pants. She paused at his fly.

"Keep going," Nate begged squeezing his fingers tighter into her hair. Kayla's fingers grazed over the soft fabric of Nate's pants, inching her way closer to the zipper. With a grin stretched out across her face, she slowly pulled down the metal binding.

Nate's pants dropped to his knees and Kayla's grin grew as she watched his cock spring up from its binding. Nate gasped as Kayla's hand curled around his shaft.

"Oh, yes, please," Nate moaned as Kayla's hand applied the pressure that Nate craved. Kayla's eyes remained locked on Nate, as his eyes roll back in his head. Kayla rubbed the tip of Nate's crown spreading his juices around the head. Each pass of her thumb over his tender flesh caused Nate to twitch.

Kayla parted her lips and sank her head down over Nate's erection. As she played with him, she ran her hands over his body feeling his smooth chiseled flesh. Deep within her, her emotions ran high. She knew her trigger to her animal nature was sex and breathed in deeply to steady herself. The last thing she wanted was to unleash the wolf in the house.

"More," Nate begged as Kayla slurped and squeezed. Never before had she wanted to please anymore more. The soft tones of Nate's voice eased her tension. Nothing else mattered to her, but Nate. All the stress concerning his father, all the tribal rules and regulations slipped away as she drove Nate's cock deeper into her throat.

Nate's fingers crunched further into Kayla's scalp, holding her in place. Slow and steady she bobbed her head allowing her saliva to lubricate his shaft. Every inch she took of him, the stronger the wolf became. She pulled herself off him and pushed her way back to the headboard.

"Give me a second," she panted trying to steady her nerves. Nate smiled as he moved off the bed allowing his jeans to hit the floor. He stood at the edge of the bed. Kayla glanced up at him as she tamed the fire that burned within her.

"You okay?" The concern in Nate's voice was sincere. He knew her struggle was real and gave her the space she needed. Once her tremors were under control, Kayla crawled to the edge of the bed and wrapped her arms around Nate's body. She leaned closer to him deliberately breathing on his neck. With her tongue stretched out, she grazed over his skin taking in his essences until she reached his earlobe. As Kayla tugged on his earlobe, Nate grabbed her and held her close.

His chest rose and fell sporadically as he panted. Kayla knew his triggers and was trying to push his buttons. A low groan resonated from the depths of his chest as his grip around Kayla drew tighter. Nate's eyes fluttered opened as she moved back from him.

"Why did you stop? That felt so good," he complained as Kayla rubbed her breasts over his body. She pressed her lips to his and embraced him passionately. Nate squeezed her body, refusing to let her go as their bodies crashed against each other.

"I want you," Nate groaned as Kayla's hand drifted from his head down his back and clenched her fingers into his buttocks.

"You have me."

"That's not what I mean."

"Nothing is stopping you." Kayla smiled as Nate tried to pull away from her embrace. Kayla held on tighter refusing to let him go. Nate wrestled Kayla to the bed, landing on her. She giggled as Nate's fingers grazed over her thighs. Kayla gasped as Nate's fingers entered her body.

"I want you," Nate repeated pumping his fingers in and out of her. "All of you, right now." Kayla's juices spilled over his fingers as he pressed his body on hers. At each pump, Kayla lost her resolve to play. The deeper Nate went, the more her body craved him. Kayla wrapped her fingers around Nate's wrists and withdrew him from her. Nate's eyebrows crunched together and concern flashed across his face. Kayla shoved on Nate's chest throwing him off her. Before Nate could protest, Kayla was on him.

"Yes," Nate hissed as Kayla shifted her body down to his waist and popped his erection back into her mouth. Greedily, Kayla took him.

"That's it, take it all," Nate groaned as he wound his arm around Kayla. The slurping noises of her sucking his cock filled the room.

"Tighter, please, squeeze that cock. Take it all," Nate pleaded as Kayla consumed and stole his attention. No longer was it just a need, the passion grew to desire. Before Kayla could overthink things, she took him out of her mouth and slipped her body over his. Kayla crawled over his legs and grabbed the shaft of Nate's cock placing it between her legs. She guided him into her eagerly awaiting body.

"Please," Nate huffed. The short whistle of air escaping Nate's lips caused Kayla to smile. As she stared down at him, she moved her hips down taking Nate's crown into her. Her body opened for him as she slipped further down consuming all of him.

"Oh, yes," Nate's eyes rolled back as Kayla shifted her hips allowing his shaft to drifted in and out of her. With each thrust, Kayla fought against the animal within her. Out of all the people she had been with, only the thickness of Nate could invoke the animal. As he hit her inner walls she shuddered.

Kayla closed her eyes allowing her other senses to take over. Nate's cock throbbed in her as she moved slow and steady. With his hands on her hips, Nate jerked his hips upward causing Kayla to slam back down on him.

"Is that how you want it?" Kayla asked as Nate's movements grew intense. Nate didn't respond. He simply held her in place as he rocked his body violently up and down pushing and pulling his cock in and out of her. Kayla's body responded as Nate's hand drifted over her stomach and grazed her inner thigh. Kayla gasped as Nate rubbed the tiny bulb between her lips. The pressure of his finger aroused her.

"Remain calm," Kayla told herself as she fought against the wolf inside her. The animal rattled its cage begging to be released as Nate's finger pressed harder. Kayla gasped for air as their bodies melded into one.

Chapter 3

As Kayla rocked, she didn't notice Nate curling his arms around her forcing her down. She kissed him tenderly as their bodies moved. The new position allowed Nate to dig deeper into her. She lifted her hand up and slammed it against the back wall to steady herself as he rammed into her. For every slam of his cock, Nate stole Kayla's breath.

Nate's cock was thick and hit every inch of Kayla. As she tried to hold back the tension grew. With each stroke, Kayla wondered how much longer she would last.

"More," Nate gurgled as his tongue stretched out eager for more. Kayla smiled as she leaned down once more, placing her hands on the wall as she dropped her body down. Nate's tongue parted Kayla's lips and rolled about her mouth as he held her.

Kayla couldn't help but be completely submersed in Nate. Everywhere she turned, he was there with his thick arms. Kayla swam in the pleasure of having Nate to herself. He was hers and she was his, there was no longer any denying it. Nate fit her like a glove and as the moonlight peaked in through the thin currents of their bedroom, Kayla knew she was home.

"You feel so good," Kayla said as Nate slowed his jerking and filled her needs. From the way his chest rose and fell, she could tell he was trying to hold off as long as he could.

"I'm glad you think so." Nate smiled into her hair as his hand cupped the back of her head, his right arm holding her in place. Before Kayla could shift her body upward, Nate pulled her to the left, and they rolled.

Kayla blinked as she realized she was no longer on top. Now, Nate was all she could see. The walls of the room where gone. As far as she knew, they were out in the woods. But the squeaky mattress that bent under their weight was a soft reminder of her surroundings.

"I love you," Nate panted as he draped Kayla's legs around his waist and dug his hard cock deeper into her. As his balls slapped her butt, Kayla scrambled to hold him with her legs. The tension in her body burned as every muscle tightened. Her fingers clawed at his back as her juices poured out of her.

"Don't hold back, let it all go."

"I can't," Kayla cried out, even as she longed to do as he said.

"Yes you can. No one will mind."

"The furniture might," Kayla gasped as Nate pushed his cock as far into her as he could go. Kayla's eyes rolled back into her head as Nate slipped his cock out slowly ensuring Kayla felt every inch of him.

A moan escaped Kayla's lips as her head flew back and her fingers dug into the sheets. There wasn't another man alive who could fill her up the way Nate did, and he knew it. Instinctively Kayla rocked her hips upward, forcing his cock to bury itself deeper inside her. Nate pushed aside Kayla's hair to reveal the pleasure etched across her face as she came.

There was no escaping the onslaught of ecstasy, once it started and Kayla knew that the tighter her body molded around Nate's cock, the more likely it was that he would come as well. Between Kayla's legs, Nate trembled as he forced himself to continue. At a final squeeze of her inner walls, Nate let out a low groan and his head dropped. Kayla reached up and brushed his hair from his beautifully sweaty face. Nate's eyes remained open, staring at Kayla as he filled her up.

"I love you. You know that?" Nate huffed as he lowered himself down to the bed beside Kayla. Kayla twisted her body towards him and brushed his cheek with the back of her hand. In the soft pale light of the moon, Kayla saw the love and admiration that filled Nate. In the depths of his eyes he saw no one but her.

"Why?"

"Because only you know how to please me," he answered as he mustered the strength to lean over and kissed Kayla tenderly. Kayla's entire being lit up as Nate filled every dark place with light and held her attention like no other.

"Maybe we can do this again tomorrow?" Kayla tried to restrain the smile that was playing at the corner of her lips as she spoke. Nate's eyebrow rose as he leaned in and pressed his lips to her forehead.

"You aren't getting out of going tomorrow, if that is what you are thinking," Nate laughed as Kayla's lips went from a smile to a pout.

"Oh, come on," Kayla grumbled as she rolled over to climb off the bed and moved towards the bathroom door. "You know how your family feels about me. I doubt they would want me there." She pushed through the bathroom door. The cool air washed over her hot skin soothing her as she walked toward the shower over the tub.

"Everyone in the tribe goes. Apparently he is making a huge announcement tomorrow, so everyone in the village will be there." Nate's voice was muffled through the half-closed door as Kayla stripped her shirt off.

"Okay, so we say we were there, but don't go," Kayla answered as the water from the faucet poured over her hand. Once the water was the right temperature, she stepped in and flicked on the shower head. The warm water washed over her body.

"Why don't you want to go?" Nate's voice droned over the tumbling water. Kayla shook her head. It wasn't that she didn't like a good party, she did. But, deep in her gut, she knew she wouldn't be welcome. After all, to Eric and Jessie she was still an outsider. Not to mention the disgust that Eric flashed at her when she was able to command the tribe's members.

"I'm just afraid they will tie me up in the barn again." Kayla knew her words were a lie. Flashes of her first meeting with Eric came into her mind as she flushed the water from her face with her hands.

"But you are one of us now. You have to come."

"I don't think Eric wants me to. Besides, I think I am coming down with something." Kayla began hacking in the shower to feign an illness. Before Kayla could laugh, the shower curtain flew back. She jumped as Nate glared at her. His eyes were focused on her face. The flash of light playing in his irises gave Kayla chills.

"You are going and that is final."

Kayla stuck out her tongue and pulled the shower curtain closed again. She knew she could use her gift to persuade him otherwise, but that wouldn't be good for her in the long run. The last time she did it, Nate found himself doing the dishes for a week.

"Fine," Kayla grunted as she heard the bathroom door close. Her shoulders dropped as her heart stammered in her chest. "I'll go, but I don't have to like it."

The creak of the bathroom door caused Kayla's lips to twitch. The room grew heavy. A dark shadow lingered behind the shower curtain and Kayla giggled.

"If you are going to get in with me, now would be the time. I'm almost done." Kayla ripped the curtain back and gasped. A young woman with long raven-black hair stood in the center of the bathroom. Kayla flicked off the water and reached for the towel.

"Can I help you?" Kayla asked looking through the crack of the bathroom door for Nate. Surely he must be pulling a prank on her. She stepped out, unashamed of her nakedness. After all, the woman was in her bathroom, what else did she expect?

"Hello?" Kayla waved her hand before the woman, but the girl did not move.

"Okay," Kayla wrapped the towel around her body and side-stepped around the girl. As Kayla pushed open the bathroom door, releasing a wave of steam into the bedroom, she turned around. The woman placed a hand on Kayla's shoulder and stared at her with eyes like an abyss.

"You are the one."

Kayla stared at the girl for what seemed like an eternity. As fear raised the hair on the back of her neck, she found she couldn't scream. Everything had melted away. The sink, the toilet, the shower, all faded into a smoky void. All that remained were Kayla and the girl.

"What do you want?" Kayla finally managed to say, as the girl removed her hand from Kayla's shoulder.

"It is set. All things will be made right by you."

"What things? What are you talking about?"

"That's a good question. Kayla? Who are you talking to?" In the blink of an eye, the girl was gone and Kayla found herself in the bathroom once again, with Nate by her side.

"You didn't just see that?" Kayla gasped as she turned to wrap her arms around Nate's neck. Fear stole the warmth from her blood, and her eyes darted around the room in search of the girl.

"See what?"

"There was a girl in the bathroom, long black hair, deep-set eyes?"

"Kayla?" Nate pulled Kayla away from him and he studied her as Kayla twitched and scanned the area.

"There is no one is here but us. I think you took too hot a shower and spooked yourself in the mirror." Nate walked over to the sink and rubbed his hand down the length of the mirror. Kayla sucked in a deep breath, as two ghostly images stared back at her - Nate and herself.

"Come on. Enough talk of tomorrow. We both need some sleep." Nate curled his arm around Kayla's waist and walked her to the bed. Kayla plopped down on the soft mattress keeping her eyes trained on the bathroom door.

"Look, if you really don't want to go tomorrow, you don't have to. I can make an excuse for why you aren't there." Nate pulled back the covers and slipped in between the sheets. Kayla rose and dropped the towel before quickly returning to the safety of Nate's arms.

"Sleep," Kayla mumbled. But she knew sleep would not visit her – not with her mind racing from her encounter. Kayla sucked in a deep breath as Nate's breathing turned into snoring.

"You are the one," the girl's voice played back in Kayla's mind as the light of the moon drifted past the window.

Chapter 4

Kayla's eyes fluttered open as the sun's light broke through her sleep. She rolled over to find Nate gone. She rubbed the sleep from her eyes and stretched shaking off her unwillingness.

"Maybe it won't be so bad," Kayla thought to herself as she climbed out of the bed. "After all, if you want to be a part of this village, you have to be social."

She rummaged through her closet and pulled out a shirt and pants. As she slipped on her shirt, her eyes darted to the bathroom door. For a split moment she wondered if what had happened last night was just a fluke. She shook her head and pushed the memory from her mind as she pulled up her pants and walked out into the living room.

"Hey there, Sleepyhead." Nate flashed his humble smile at her as he pulled out plates from the cabinets above the sink. Kayla walked into the kitchen, keeping her eyes locked on Nate as he moved about the kitchen.

"Are you hungry? I made breakfast."

"After last night, you know it."

Nate's smile grew wide, as he sat the plates down and retrieved glasses. Kayla watched as he poured orange juice and handed the glasses to her. Kayla set them on the small table as Nate joined her, carrying two plates stacked with food.

Together, they sat down. Kayla sucked in the aroma of crisp bacon before glancing over at Nate. He was staring at her with wide eyes, waiting for her to begin.

"I was thinking about last night," Kayla said grabbing a strip of bacon and popping it into her mouth. The moment Kayla began eating, so did Nate. She watched as he piled the eggs onto his fork and shoveled them into his mouth. Nate grunted as Kayla watched him. Her eyebrow rose with amusement as she watched him devour his plate in seconds flat.

"What about last night? I thought you enjoyed yourself?"

"Not the sex, about the party tonight."

"Oh?" Nate wiped the corner of his lips with his sleeve and sat back in his chair.

"Maybe I should go."

"I knew you would come around."

"What time does it start?" Kayla asked, picking at her eggs while a feeling nagged at her stomach. Despite the fact that she was famished, her nerves were too wound up to allow her to eat.

"Remember? It is sort of an all-day thing."

Kayla dropped her fork as the words spilled from his lips. "All day?"

Nate nodded forcing another bite of food into his already jammed packed mouth.

"Traditions. Every year a speech is given. I think Eric goes a little over board with them, so we don't have to be there till noon." Kayla glanced at the clock above the stove. The hands ticked away as fear gripped her.

"That's in fifteen minutes."

"Well then, you should probably hurry up and eat or we'll be late."

"But?" Kayla had thought she would have more time, but now found herself out of it. It didn't help that the butterflies floating around in her stomach swirled like a twister inside her. Suddenly, the smell of bacon wasn't so pleasant. Kayla bolted from the table and rushed to the bathroom.

"You okay?" Nate's voice was muffled from the other side of the bathroom door as she expelled what little she had in her. Kayla grunted as she hovered over the toilet.

Once the last bit of food was no longer in her, Kayla sat back. Sweat dripped off her brow and her vision blurred. The creak of the bathroom door startled her and her eyes shifted to the dark figure in the doorway. Fear stole the warmth from her as she tried to scramble to the nook between the toilet and the bath tub.

"Kayla? You sure you're okay?"

"I don't think so." As Kayla's eyes focused, she exhaled. Nate crouched down and lifted her off the floor.

"If going to the party is going to make you this upset, then maybe we shouldn't go."

"You should." Kayla huffed as Nate helped her to her feet. With Nate's arms around her waist, she moved to the sink. Frosty water poured out of the tap like a waterfall. Kayla shoved her hands under the running water and splashed her face to cool the fire of her skin.

"But I don't want to leave you like this."

"Take me to Alice's. I will get some rest there."

"Why not stay here?" Kayla's heart dropped at the thought of spending time alone in his house. She had spent more time here than anywhere else in the village. But still, the idea of being here alone scared the crap out of her. She shook her head in protest. She would rather go to the party than be left alone here.

"Maybe going will be better."

"Will you make up your mind?"

Kayla pulled a towel from the rack and wiped the water from her face before turning around to turn off the tap. As she turned to face Nate again, her stomach shifted as her eyes darted around the room. If she could hold down the contents in her stomach, she would be fine. She sucked in a deep breath to steady her nerves.

The concern on Nate's face bothered her. Did she dare tell him her fear? Would he think her crazy? She didn't care. All she knew is that his home was no longer the safe haven it once was - every fiber in her being screamed at her to leave. Although the sun light poured in through the windows, the shadows grew. Kayla's eyes shifted to them as if they were calling her name. She clung to Nate waiting for the vision of the woman to return.

"Let's go. Now." Kayla whispered into Nate's ear. She wondered if he could hear the fear she was so desperately trying to hide. Nate squeezed her tighter as if trying to keep the pieces of her together.

"Brush your teeth first," Nate suggested as he let her go. "Then we can go."

Chapter 5

Kayla moved quickly down the steps and stood by the jeep waiting for Nate to unlock it for her. Her foot tapped as her body sparked with electricity. She stared at the house like it was a trap, she was half expecting to see someone peering back at her through the windows.

The click of the doors unlocking caused her to jump and the sound of Nate's laugh threw her off.

"Are you sure you're okay?" he asked again as Kayla pulled open the car door, and slipped in. For some reason the thought being inside the jeep gave her the security she needed. She didn't speak for fear of her words giving her away, so she nodded.

" You've been on edge from the moment you woke up. What's going on?" The rumble of the engine soothed her and as the jeep pulled away from the house, the pressure around Kayla lifted. She sucked in a deep breath and held it for a moment before letting it escape.

"You will think I am crazy," Kayla mumbled as she twisted her fingers around in her lap.

"Well, that is a given. You are a girl. Crazy is to be expected."

"No. I mean clinically crazy."

"Kayla?" Nate shifted his gaze from the road to Kayla and back again. She could feel the questions in his mind and wondered what he would think if she told him. The idea was foreign even to her. But still she couldn't shake the image from last night.

"Never mind. It was probably just a bad dream or something."

"If it is bothering you this much, you should tell someone."

Kayla shook her head and pressed her lips together. The further they got from his house, the better she felt. The twisting inside her stomach was nearly gone by the time they reached the outskirt of town.

"I'll be okay," Kayla said as the town drew closer. "Maybe this party is a good idea after all."

"The moment you feel uncomfortable we can leave okay?"

"Sure." Kayla turned her head and let the scenery pass by her. The dark-green of the forest faded as shops and houses filtered through. Kayla sat up straight as they pulled into the center of town.

"Wow."

"I know right? Alice wasn't kidding when she said everyone would be here."

Kayla's eyes drifted through the sea of faces - everyone who lived within a fifty-mile radius had come out. Families and friends, and people she had never even seen before wandered through the streets. Nate weaved around the pedestrians and inched his way closer to the center. Every parking spot was filled and every inch of the street was filled with booths.

"What kind of party is this? I thought it was supposed to be Eric's birthday." Kayla asked as she noticed vendors and crafts set up in the open alleyways.

"It is. But you can also call it a tribal meeting. Folks from all around come once a year to pay their respects to my dad."

"Wow. No wonder the man hates me."

Nate laughed but his eyes drifted to Kayla. "Why do you say that?"

"Think about it. I am the only one who hasn't shown him the respect he thinks he deserves."

"And that is why I love you so much. Eric thinks that because he is the tribal leader, he should automatically get respect. But respect is earned, not given."

Kayla reached out her hand and squeezed Nate's. She flashed a tiny smile as his words rang true. "I knew there was a reason I liked you."

"Ah, finally." Nate slipped his hand away from Kayla and turned the wheel. His little jeep maneuvered perfectly into the last spot. Nate killed the engine and shifted in his seat to face Kayla.

"Feeling any better?"

"A little. The fresh air will do me good."

"Then come on. We have things to see and I have you to do."

"Excuse me?" Kayla smiled as she caught Nate's snide comment.

Nate smiled as he leaned in closer to Kayla. As his lips brushed against hers he whispered, "Come on, haven't you ever had sex in public?"

Kayla kissed him and reached for the door handle. As the door opened, Kayla slipped out leaving Nate befuddled. She laughed as she closed the door keeping her eyes locked on him.

"Maybe later," Nate chuckled as he climbed out and met her on the sidewalk.

"Maybe. But I wouldn't hold your breath."

"You are such a tease."

"And you like it like that," Kayla giggled as she tugged on Nate's arm and led him through the crowded street.

Everywhere she turned, Kayla found something to marvel at. Trinkets and food filled every bit of her senses and pushed aside her fears. The longer she stayed engaged and entertained the further the vision of the girl drifted away.

"Wait, I want to show you something." Nate stopped at a small booth in the back of the alley. Kayla skipped to his side and her eyes widened. The booth showcased different handcrafted necklaces and various forms of jewelry. As her eyes drifted over the merchandise, she came up short when Nate held up a stunning necklace.

"That is amazing." Kayla reached up and with the slightest touch traced the stone set in an intricate pattern of woven silver. As the sun hit the stone, it shimmered. Every color of the rainbow filled the small gem.

"The stone is an opal."

"That is gorgeous."

"I'm glad you think so. I had Keeti here make it for you." Kayla's eyes shifted to the girl behind the booth. She stared at Kayla with wonder and fascination. Kayla's lips twitched as she smiled at the girl.

"Thank you. But, I thought you were supposed to give presents to the birthday boy, not me."

"Well, it can be our secret." Nate said as he motioned for Kayla to turn. She twisted around as Nate slipped the necklace around her and clasped it.

"There, now there will be a reason for people to stare at you."

"She doesn't need that to have people stare," Keeti spoke. Kayla glanced at her as her tiny voice chimed like bells. "She is stunning even without the necklace."

"Um, thank you." Kayla tried not to let the embracement reach her cheeks, but her face grew hot despite her efforts.

"You are the one," Keeti said as she bowed her head low.

"What? What did you just say?" Kayla's heart pounded in her ears. The fear crept up her spin setting her on edge as Nate smiled at her.

"She just means for me. You are the one for me."

Kayla brushed her fingertips over the stone as she tried to calm herself. But the shadows she fought so hard to vanquish pushed themselves into the light.

"Thank you for the necklace, but I can't accept this."

"Too late. It's bought and paid for."

"Nate, please."

Kayla lifted her hands up trying to get the necklace unlatched to give it back, but it was no use. Her fingers were too nervous and her palms too sweaty to get a good grip on it.

"It isn't an engagement ring, relax." Nate grabbed Kayla's hands and held them as he looked at her. Deep within his eyes, Kayla found the peace she needed. As her heart sputtered, she breathed in and out.

"Keeti, thank you for the necklace. Now do you have the gift for my father?" Nate asked turning his attention back to the girl behind the booth. Keeti nodded and took two small boxes from under the table, setting them down in front of her.

"Very special. Be sure to present last," Keeti tapped on the box to her left as she continued to stare at Kayla. "He will be impressed."

"Excellent. Thank you so much." The smile on Nate's face glowed as he picked up the boxes. "Come on. Let's see if this won't get you favor with my dad."

Kayla stole one last glimpse of Keeti before she turned and followed Nate back down the alley. As she walked she noticed more eyes shifted her way.

"It's the necklace," she reminded herself as she caught up with Nate.

"There you are! I was wondering if you would show up." Alice's bright face filled Kayla with joy. Even if others stared at her, with Alice there, Kayla didn't feel so secluded.

"What a stunning necklace," Alice's eyes widened as she spotted the stone around Kayla's neck. Alice shook her head as she peeled her eyes away from the rainbow opal, toward Nate. "Your dad is looking for you."

"I thought so. Here," Nate pushed one of the boxes to Kayla forcing her to take it.

"Give this to him. Trust me; he is going to love it."

"But?"

"No but's. Just do it." Nate's eyebrows pulled together as he pleaded with Kayla. "For me?"

"For you." Kayla gave in and she wondered what Nate had bought for his dad. Alice beamed with excitement as she scooped her arm around Kayla's and pulled her to the center of the crowd.

"Adam is about to go on stage now," Alice informed them as they weaved through the mass of people moving closer to the stage.

"Adam is going to retell the history of our tribe and I want you front and center," Alice said as the crowd parted and Kayla noticed a row of seats not yet filled, in the front.

"Ooh, right there," Alice pointed to the front row center chairs. Kayla sighed as she followed Alice and sat down. The wooden stage before her was enormous. Kayla's eyes shifted around as she tried to get her bearings.

"The show will begin in a minute, so don't go anywhere." Alice smiled as Nate took his place beside Kayla.

"I am going to get Jessie and tell him the show is about to start. He always loves hearing this story. I'll be right back." Alice disappeared quickly into the crowd leaving Kayla and Nate alone.

"A bit over the top, but that is how my father wanted it," Nate grumbled as he got settled into his seat.

"He wanted all this?" Kayla's eyes shifted to the crowd surrounding them. While not everyone glanced her way, several paused and stared at her, beside Nate.

"He likes to remind people of how important he is. But don't let that ruin the experience. Our history really is quiet magical, to say the least."

Kayla shifted in her seat and set the box under her chair. As the curtain of the stage opened, Kayla glanced at the man towering above her. His deep-set eyes held her attention as the music filled the area. For a moment Kayla forgot all about the crowd around her. Her mind slipped as the drums pounded to the rhythm of her heart.

Chapter 6

"On the last night of summer, many moons ago," the performer began and Kayla was mesmerized by him. The way his muscle flexed as he drifted to the edge of the stage holding everyone's attention.

"That's Adam, can you believe it?" Nate whispered trying not to break the spell that Adam was weaving. Kayla's eyes barely shifted to Nate as he spoke, but the name was familiar. Was this the same Adam she had met when she first came here? He seemed taller and more defined now, or maybe it was the stage and costumes, that made him look that way.

Kayla didn't really care. She leaned forward, taking in every word as if it were life itself and only he could give it to her.

"A babe cried in the straw as his mother Naku, slipped from this world." Behind Adam several actors appeared on the stage setting the scene for the audience. A young girl remained in the back weeping as the child cried out.

"The loss of his mother, Naku, drove a wedge between the boy, Toko, and his father, Tokomu, the chief of this tribe."

Kayla's eyes shifted to the taller man playing Tokomu. The dark make-up made his face stern and mean. Kayla shuddered as the image of the woman came back to her. She jolted back in her seat as the young woman moved around the background. Kayla reached for Nate's wrist and gripped it tight.

"As the years passed, the boy cried out for a way to help his father see him as a man. And the spirits answered."

A swirl of wind kicked up around the stage as more characters raced about the area. Kayla's eyes were transfixed on the woman in the back, however. Her blood ran cold as the woman gazed at her. In the midst of the commotion on stage, Kayla barely heard her speak.

"Take your place, child," she said over Adam's monologue. Kayla glanced at Nate wondering if he to saw what she was seeing. But Nate showed no signs of noticing the woman; he was too involved with the other players.

"The spirit of the wolf came to Toko and entered him," Adam continued as the woman glared at him, shaking her head disapprovingly. The crowd around Kayla cheered as the wolf transformed into Eric.

"Today, fathers pass their gifts to their sons and so it has been since the moment Toko cried out to the spirits. It was his prayer that gave us this blessing," Eric announced as the crowd's noise died down. Kayla shot Nate a glance as Eric's eyes drifted over them. Nate smiled and nodded once before turning to his right.

"My son," Eric lifted his hands up, as the woman circled around Eric grimacing. Kayla's eyes darted back to Nate, but it wasn't Nate who rose from his chair. Jessie stood next to Nate and for a moment Kayla wondered how Jessie got there. She shook her head trying to recall seeing Jessie, but all that consumed her mind was the woman on the stage taunting Eric.

"Evil, despiser, interloper," the woman hissed above the crowd. Kayla's grip on Nate grew tighter as Eric continued.

"My eldest, will take my place as your tribe leader."

The crowd cheered as Jessie climbed on stage to join his father. "As it was from the beginning, so it shall continue. The tribe will go on and Jessie will be your new chief." Eric wrapped his hand around Jessie's arm and raised it into the sky.

The woman on stage hissed and flew towards Kayla stopping inches from her face. The woman's dark eyes glared through Kayla as she hissed. "Take your place."

Kayla could no longer hold her fear and shot up out of her chair screaming, "NO!"

The crowd stopped cheering, as the woman vanished from Kayla's sight. The silence startled her and Kayla scanned the crowd realizing their silence had been caused by her.

"Who are you to challenge the chief?" Jessie demanded slipping his hand from Eric's.

"I..." Kayla's eyes danced around the sea of faces until they landed on Nate. His eyes stared up at her with a pain that stabbed into her heart.

"No, I just..." Kayla mumbled trying to find the words, but panic stole her speech. Without another word Kayla took off pushing through the crowd.

Her face burned with embarrassment as she tried to keep her tears at bay. The moment she broke from the crowd, she shifted and pushed herself towards the forest.

As the light of the sun faded between the thick of the trees, Kayla's heart broke. She knew she would never be able to go back. If Eric disliked her before, she was certain he hated her now.

Kayla pushed further into the forest letting all else slip away.

"Being a wolf wouldn't be so bad," she thought as her nails racked against the soft soil beneath her. Without another thought, Kayla pushed herself further until the whiff of meat crossed her path. She slowed and saw lights from a fire up ahead.

"Who, in the world, would be out this far?"

She slowed her pace and walked closer as the smell of meat and herbs filled her nostrils. In the thick of the trees, Kayla noticed a small hut with a single fire burning brightly outside. A tall man paced around the flames as cries of pain filled the area. Kayla paused and waited as the wind kicked up around her.

Then, curiosity stabbed at her, causing her to inch closer. Before she knew it, Kayla was by the window of the small hut looking in. She gasped to see the same woman as before, on a mat of straw pushing life into this world.

Chapter 7

Kayla watched as the midwives inside the hut scrambled for the essentials to clean the child. The young woman with long hair as black as a crow's feathers panted on the mats as the pressure ceased.

"Tell, me," the woman cried. "Is he okay?"

"She, is just fine." The midwife held the child up to the woman on the mat. The moment their eyes met, the young woman's heart filled with joy. The baby pulled in her first breath before bellowing out with its new lungs. The cries of the child filled the small house and relief came over the women inside.

Kayla couldn't help but smile as she watched the scene unfold. Hope and joy filled her as she pressed her wolf's snout against the window. For a moment she wondered if she was intruding, but the thought faded the moment she saw the baby's face.

"She is strong and will lead us well," the midwife exclaimed tucking the child into a fresh blanket. The babe's cries died out as the midwife wrapped the child up into a tight roll. A young man poked his head into the hut with eager eyes. The midwife held the girl up allowing him to see his new child.

"Matoki," the young man whispered in awe before his eyes flashed to his wife on the mats. The midwife turned towards the new mother. With arms stretched out, the young mother paused and a new pain shot through her hips and belly. Taking the child from its mother, the midwife passed the baby to another so she could attend to the woman on the mat.

"What is this?" Reaching down to the young woman, the midwife pulled forth another child.

"A boy!" the midwife cried out with joy, seeing that the young boy didn't need the same care his sister had required. The young mother huffed and puffed straining to see the second child as the midwife swaddled him.

Kayla gasped as she saw the second child. Side by side the babies were identical in every way. Kayla panted for the new mother as the news hit them both.

"You have been blessed by the spirits. Your house has now two new mouths to feed."

"What?!" The door flew open to the hut and the young man raced in to see for himself. With wide eyes he almost stumbled when he saw a son in the arms of the midwife.

"Naku," the young man's gaze drifted to his wife. Kayla's eyes popped opened as her mouth dropped. She shook her head trying to understand what it was she was seeing.

"How is this even possible?" Kayla wondered as her eyes remained fixed on the woman on the mat. She didn't appear to be the same tormented spirit that had been haunting her for the past twenty-four-hours. No, this woman was tender and kind.

Kayla pulled her gaze from Naku and stared at the man. The smile on his face reached his eyes as he extended his hands to his son to hold him.

"Tokomu, meet Toko," Naku's voice cracked as she stared at her husband and new son. The midwife turned to collect Matoki from the second midwife and handed the young babe to her mother. Kayla remained frozen by the window spying on the family as both parents cuddled their children in their arms.

"He will lead the tribe," Tokomu announced, his eyes trained on the young boy in his arms.

"But Matoki was first-born," Naku stated glancing at the sober faces of the midwives for confirmation. "Even you saw her first."

"But she is not suited to lead this tribe. Toko will lead. He will be strong and wise. He will possess the skills needed to survive the winters and bring our tribe to fertile lands."

"That is not the way of our tribe. The first born has those rights. You cannot take them from her."

Tokomu glared at his wife, still lying on the mats and pulled his son closer to his chest. "You will do as I say. Be glad that you have a daughter to carry on your traditions, for this boy shall carry on mine." With that Tokomu pulled open the door and disappeared into the night.

With tears in her eyes, Naku brushed her fingertips over the young girl's face. As the child nestled into her bosom, Naku sighed.

Rage filled Kayla as she watched Naku with her new daughter. Every emotion that flowed through Naku, Kayla felt. From the joy of the child in her arms to the hatred of Tokomu for stealing what was rightfully hers.

Kayla tried to pull away, but was caught up in the moment. She had the power to rip that man to shreds, but found herself stuck by the window as a mere observer.

"Tokomu is right. So many others who have tried for children have not been blessed the way you have. Take heed, young Naku, both your children have a part to play in the grand scheme of things."

"It is not fair that my husband would deny Matoki her rightful future."

"Then go to the spirits and ask for guidance. They will answer your pleas."

Kayla shook her head in sync with Naku's. "Yes," they said together. "I will do that."

The sights of the hut and the smell of meat faded with the vision, as a new one formed before her. Kayla blinked as she saw a shadow figure drifting through the trees. Instinctively she pushed off and raced after it only to come to a sudden stop.

In a clearing of the forest Kayla watched as Naku sat with nothing but a fire burning before her. The flames licked her face as the woman rocked back and forth in prayer. Kayla inched closer to get a better view and ducked around the fallen tree as the prayer rose higher with the flames of the fire.

The sun came and went; still Kayla remained with the woman. She waited patiently for something as Naku's cries continued. Then, out of the trees a gray wolf emerged. Kayla jumped up ready to strike it down, to protect Naku, but found herself unable to move once again.

The gray wolf towered above Naku as she sat on the forest floor. Kayla could sense Naku's fear and wondered what was to become of the poor girl. Her heart raced as Naku's eyes widened with fear wondering if the wolf was there to claim her life.

Scrambling to find a weapon, Naku scrabbled through the leaves and branches until her fingers gripped a sharp stone. She raised the crude blade up to the wolf and Kayla growled.

"Be still and listen." A voice on the wind howled through the trees, as it rustled the branches and leaves. Naku and Kayla stared at the wolf in wonder as it sat beside her with its head raised high and proud.

"Your pleas have been heard," the voice announced as Kayla and Naku's hearts raced within their chests.

Naku's eyes darted to and fro searching for the origins of the voice, but she saw nothing and no one except for the wolf.

"The fate of your tribe has been decided."

"But?" Naku began to protest as the wolf lay down beside her and nuzzled its head into her lap. Fearful, Naku glanced down to see her children in her lap instead of the mighty wolf. Naku wrapped her children in her arms and sobbed.

Kayla held her ground waiting and hoping for the chance to strike. But the sight of the babies in Naku's lap confused her. Only when the children disappeared did Naku move. Kayla moved with her keeping to the shadows of the forest until they reached the hut once again.

"What have you done?" Tokomu demanded as Naku reached their home. Kayla growled as the hair on her back rose. Before Kayla could spring into action, Tokomu ripped out of his human form and sprang towards Naku. The yelps of tiny wolves faded as the vision drifted into the night.

"Now you know," Naku's voice startled Kayla causing her to jump. Kayla whipped her head around to see the young woman standing beside her.

"I don't understand," Kayla thought as Naku's voice spoke in her head.

"Yes you do. You are the one."

"But I am not your daughter."

"No, but you are of my daughter's blood. You are the one who is to be chief of this tribe, not that naysayer."

"Eric?"

"That man who calls himself the leader."

"There is no way for me to challenge him. I can barely shift and he is ten times stronger."

"Challenge the heir. The status of the chief is to be passed down by blood, not by rights. Challenge him and you will have the victory, for I will help you."

"I don't want to be the chief." Kayla said as the woman vanished before her eyes. Kayla shook her head trying to make sense of all that she had seen. Her heart broke as she saw Naku's body resting by her paws, slain at the hands of her husband. Kayla dropped to the ground weeping but Naku's body faded into shadow.

Once her last tear was spent, Kayla drifted to sleep on the forest floor. The darkness shrouded her and pulled her into a deep slumber. For once Kayla allowed the nothingness to overtake her.

Chapter 8

As the light of dawn filtered through her eyes, Kayla stirred. Soft, tender lips pressed against her forehead. Her skin tingled as fingertips brushed against her skin.

"Kayla?" The voice was faint as it pulled Kayla out of the darkness.

She moaned as she tried to remain in the nothingness. She knew the moment her eyes opened, the world would be there waiting for her, but she didn't want to see it just yet. She wanted the peace that surrounded her. What came with the morning was what she dreaded. Naku would be there if she wasn't already. And the accusations of the tribe would begin.

"Kayla," the voice cooed in her ear. Kayla rolled over trying to keep the darkness around her. But it wasn't the night that embraced her. Instead, it was strong arms and a familiar scent. She nuzzled her face into the nook keeping the light of the sun at bay.

"No." Kayla grumbled as she wrapped her arms around the body that held her.

"Oh thank God," Nate's voice whispered. "I thought I was going to lose you there for a minute."

Kayla's eyes fluttered open for a moment only to see Nate's dark skin of surrounding her. "Why didn't you just leave me in the forest?"

"I have been out looking for you all night."

"Why?"

"You silly girl, I told you. If you run, I run. When you took off yesterday, I didn't know where you went. I thought you might have gone back to my place, but when you weren't there, I tracked you. What were you doing in the middle of the forest?"

"Nothing," Kayla lied trying to force the images of Naku out of her mind. But, no matter what she did, the images were permanently burned into her thoughts. Kayla shifted her body pulling Nate closer to keep the light from entering.

"Kayla, what is going on? I know something is up. Please, just talk to me."

Kayla's heart thundered in her ears and her head was splitting. Every inch of her body ached. She knew Nate would continue with the questions if she didn't change the subject. It was his fingertips brushing over her bare shoulder as he spoke that tickled her fancy. Despite her attempts to remain secluded, Kayla knew only one thing that would keep her from feeling the anxiety of the world around her.

    Kayla pressed her lips to Nate as she sucked in his scent. Her fingers traced the curve of his chest. The heat from his body burned, but at least she felt something. Inside of her was numb and Kayla realized she needed to feel something – some kind of hope that things could be better.

    She rested her head on his chest and focused on his breathing as she tried to push all other thoughts from her mind. When he inhaled, she inhaled and she followed his pattern of breathing until she felt calm and still. Kayla's fingers began to wander over his chest. She opened her eyes and watched as her fingers traced the valley of his muscles through his shirt.

    Nate grabbed her hand and laid it flat on his chest. The beating of his heart was soothing, yet the fire had been kindled just as Kayla had hoped and she wanted more.

    "Kayla," his voice broke as she scooted her face closer to his.

"Don't you want this?" she asked pulling her hand away from his. Fingertips have memories, and she wanted to remember every inch of him and nothing else. She wanted him to ease the pain and make the world cease to be.

As her surroundings grew clearer in her eyes, Kayla realized Nate had brought her back to his place. She sighed forcing all other thoughts from her mind. At least for now the visions ceased.

Kayla ran her fingers down the length of him until they stopped at the seam of his pants. His breath grew shallow as if plunging into icy waters. He knew what was coming, what Kayla wanted.

She moved over him straddling him between her legs as she tugged at his pants to undo the button holding them around him. Nate stared up at her as she fumbled with the button refusing to stop her. With a swift tug, Kayla pulled his pants down and tossed them over her shoulder. She leaned down and caressed him with a hunger she hadn't felt in years. There was nothing in the world that could pull her out of this now and so she continued.

Kayla ran her tongue over Nate's nipples before opening her mouth to take him. Her fingers clawed at his skin as she tried to consume more. With every inch Nate gave her, Kayla stole a mile until her hand was around his thick cock.

She felt his heartbeat through the veins pulsing with desire. As her body shifted, Nate's hands were on her, roaming freely. He leaned closer as Kayla arched her back to take in much needed air. Before Kayla could protest, Nate's open mouth was on her breasts. His tongue swirled around her nipple sending tingles of pleasure jolting through her body. Every nerve was on fire as Nate suckled one, then the other breast.

Kayla pulled away to steal a glance at him. Lust burned in his eyes that hid his concern for her. Kayla didn't bother to look deeper, she knew what she wanted. She scooted down and dropped her body onto the firm mattress. Before Nate could say a word or try to stop her, Kayla opened her mouth and her fingers wrapped around him. He shifted his weight as Kayla tried to take all of him. The deeper she let it go down her throat, the more he twitched with pleasure.

Kayla reached up with her free hand to shove Nate's hand away from her. She didn't want any distractions as she took what she wanted. It didn't take long for Nate to get the hint and he moved his arms up over his head allowing Kayla the freedom to do what she wanted.

He kept his hands up over his head and remained still as Kayla worked on him, massaging his manhood with her tongue. Every so often her fingers found their way up to his chest and back down again. His body under Kayla's touch trembled as he moaned.

From the depths of her being a fire ignited. The tiny spark soon grew into a full-fledged wildfire that began to consume every inch of her. As she pulled his cock out of her mouth, Kayla looked up at him. His eyes were on her watching every move she made. A faint smile pulled up at the corners of his lips. It became very clear he wasn't about to make her stop.

"Kayla," his voice barely audible. "I love you."

Kayla pushed down on him swallowing every inch of his shaft that she could. The low rumble from his chest was almost a growl as she pulled him out of her mouth once again. Kayla kept her hands wrapped around his long thick shaft as she moved her hand up and down.

"Do you now?"

He propped himself up on his elbows, "Yes."

Before Kayla could stop him, his arms were around her waist, and she tumbled onto her back as Nate took his place on top of her. Kayla felt the throbbing between her legs as he inched his way towards her center. Nate paused and stared at her. Kayla wondered if he was toying with her or if the sadness in his eyes would get the better of him.

"Please," Kayla begged. Nate's eyes roamed over her body, before landing once more on Kayla's face. His eyes bore into her searching for any signs of weakness as he moved his hand down to direct his rod. Kayla sucked in a shallow breath through her teeth anticipating what came next. First, the crown of his cock pushed through Kayla's wet lips before penetrating her. Every inch of Nate spread her open as her body adjusted for more. Kayla's body took him all and Nate groaned as his head dropped and his eyes closed.

Kayla twisted her head and pressed her lips to his arm as it trembled under his weight. Her gentle kiss awoke him as he paused to stare at her for a moment. Kayla's body couldn't handle the delay. She needed him now more than ever. She lifted her hips to force him to move. When he didn't, she wrapped her legs around his body and took what she wanted. From deep within her body, Kayla felt his cock throbbing as it rubbed against her inner walls. The sensation drove her mad as she scrambled to take more.

"Squeeze me," Nate pleaded as Kayla's arms flew around his neck to hold him to her.

He kissed her, slipping his tongue inside her mouth. As their tongues flirted, he held her closer. The sensation wasn't like the fire Kayla had felt before. He was moving cautiously ensuring she felt every inch of him. Kayla didn't want him like this. She wanted it hard and rough. She wanted him to use her and to drown out the torment that was raging inside her mind.

Kayla pushed her hips hard into his forcing him deeper into her. Her nails racked his back as she moved faster.

"Not like that," he said as he raised himself up. "I know you are hurting and I don't want you to feel that way right now." He leaned down pushing Kayla's body to the mattress as his lips to graze over Kayla's neck.

"Please," Kayla begged as her hips jolted up and down causing the mattress to squeak. Nate lifted his head, his eyes peered down at her and he brushed the hair from her face. His eyes remained locked on her as he pushed himself deeper before pulling out. Kayla's body rocked with the motion as he took away her pain.

Nate shoved his hips harder and harder into Kayla's. Each thrust dug his penis deeper until Kayla had no choice but to let him have his way. With her legs locked around him, she let him take her.

"Yes," Kayla hissed as each jolt of Nate's body forced the air from her lungs. The bed slammed against the wall as Kayla's fingers dug into Nate as he jabbed and jolted with fearlessness.

His final thrust into her unhinged her body. With the explosion of passion, she felt something once again. Instead of the pain, there was pleasure. Instead of the emptiness, there was him. He brushed the loose strands away from her face and leaned into her. When their lips collided, his words seeped into Kayla's mind. Maybe he was right about things getting better. Maybe there was a way for her to go on.

Nate panted as he crumbled to the mattress. His body trembled like thunder in the valley.

"Is that what you wanted?" He asked between quick breaths. Kayla nodded as she stared up to the ceiling.

"Now are you going to tell me what is going on?"

"Nothing is going on."

"Kayla?" Nate pulled himself out of her and rolled onto his back. The heat of his naked flesh against Kayla's body soothed her. She didn't want this moment to end. She pressed herself into him, curling around his body and forcing her to mold to him. She wanted to seep into him, to be buried in him and hidden from the rest of the world.

Chapter 9

"You can't just use sex to forget things. You have to tell me what is going on."

Kayla rolled over, turning her back to him as thoughts of last night came back to haunt her. Nate lifted his hand and rubbed her back and Kayla fought the tears from starting.

"I..." Kayla started, but as the words formed in her head, she knew they were crazy.

"What?"

"I'm seeing things."

The bed shifted as Nate pulled up to rest on his elbow. Kayla didn't have to turn around to know what the look on his face would be. She had already seen the expression on her own face in the mirror.

"What kind of things?"

Kayla shook her head and she hid her face in the pillow refusing to look at him. The emotions spilled over and tears poured out of her eyes. Suddenly, Nate's rubbing stopped and the bed squeaked. Kayla knew by the sudden firmness that Nate was no longer beside her. She peeled the pillow from her head to see where he had gone. To her surprise Nate was beside her. His big gray eyes were filled with concern as his fingers ran through her hair.

"Kayla, what kind of things are you seeing?"

"I don't know. A woman, a young woman."

"Did she give you a name?"

"Naku."

The shock on Nate's face caused Kayla to shove her head back into the pillow to drown herself in the darkness once again.

"You have to tell me everything. Leave nothing out."

"No." Kayla's voice was muffled from the pillow as she spoke, but Nate ripped the pillow from her exposing her to the light.

"This is no joking matter. If Naku is communicating with you, you have to tell me."

"Why? She is just a myth, a legend, a ghost." Kayla wailed as her words streamed together. She fought back the tears begging to be released. "Why is she communicating with me?"

Calmness came over Nate and a small smile tugged at the corner of his lips. He brushed the back of his hand over Kayla's burning face.

"She is our ancestor and they only speak to those who are the rightful leaders of this tribe." Nate's voice was soothing and his eyes once filled with concern now filled with hope.

"If she is talking to you, then it is you who must lead this tribe."

"No. Eric has made it clear that Jessie is to do that."

"But you have alpha blood in you. Jessie doesn't."

"What are you talking about? Eric is the leader, Jessie is your brother, and that's just the way it will be."

"No. My family was picked once yours died. But now that you are back, you have to challenge my brother for the position."

"I don't want it."

"I don't want you to have it either, but the spirits won't rest until you give them what they want."

Kayla shook her head as Nate's words filled her mind. There was no way she could be the leader. It didn't matter that her commands were to be followed. She didn't want the responsibility.

"Come on, get dressed. We have to talk to Eric."

"No."

"Kayla, I love you. But, you have to go. If you don't do it yourself, then I will pick you up and carry you."

Kayla flew up with narrowed eyes. The thought of Nate forcing her to do anything was a blow to her. She shook her head as her lips drew into a tight line.

"You wouldn't dare."

"Don't make this difficult then."

"You will not take me anywhere." Her voice went deep as she gave the command. Nate twitched as the order was given and he knew he wouldn't be able to make her do anything.

"You want to play like that?" He hissed. "I'm just trying to help you."

"No you are taking away my freedom so I am taking away yours."

"You're about to cross a line with me," Nate warned.

"You have already done so with me," Kayla huffed as she threw the sheets off her and stood up. Her eyes scanned the room and landed on a pile of her clothes. She walked over and pulled on what she needed before turning to Nate.

"Do not follow me, do you understand?" Kayla's command was absolute and Nate's body trembled under the order. He dropped to his knees and bowed as Kayla stormed out of the room. The moment she was outside, she sucked in a deep breath. She glanced around the area. Only the tall trees of the forest welcomed her with open arms. She took off towards the forest as a howl ripped through the small house behind her.

Kayla raced through the thick brush trying to put as much space as she could between Nate and her. With each step her heart broke. She knew she crossed a line by forcing him to stay, but he had too. As she tried to keep herself together the crunching of footsteps caught her attention. Kayla paused to find Jessie and Eric hot on her trail.

"Dammit." For a moment she thought of shifting. The idea of turning wolf now was appealing, but she knew she couldn't out run them. She turned and remained still, as she waited for them to come.

"Where is Nate?" Jessie demanded and he stopped short when he saw was Kayla alone. Kayla glared at him knowing he had no power over her.

"Kayla, we heard Nate's howl. So, where is he?"

"Back at his place I would assume," she spit the words back at them as Eric began to circle her.

"You *assume*?" Jessie crossed his arms waiting for her to cave.

"That's where I left him. What he does when he isn't with me is not my concern anymore."

"I take it you two had a fight, then?" Eric pressed in closer closing the gap between them. Kayla's eyes shifted to the old man as he moved around her.

"Maybe."

"Why? What was your fight about?" Jessie asked keeping his eyes locked on Kayla.

"That is none of your business."

"Nate is my business," Eric snapped, And he rushed Kayla, only to stop inches from her face. In the depths of his eyes Kayla saw the hatred burning like a raging inferno. She wondered just how much kindling she would need to throw on that flame to cause him to explode. The hairs on her neck rose as she felt her body itching for the fight.

"Tell me why my son howled the way he did."

"Go ask him yourself. I am certain he would love for you to know." Kayla grunted as Eric moved back and studied her.

"Maybe we will." Eric nodded to Jessie and without a single word being exchanged; Jessie took off, running towards Nate's.

"You think you can just come around here and disrupt this tribe?"

"You want me gone, I get it. Now, I don't have a reason to stay."

"Then it's over between you and my son?" Kayla noticed the spark of joy quenching the rage within his eyes. She knew Eric would love nothing more than for her to leave.

"Yes."

"Then go. I won't stop you. But if you ever show your face around here again."

"You have no power over me old man and you know it. The only one who did is long gone now, so don't make empty threats you can't back up."

"My threats are never empty, little girl, and even if you have the power to control MY tribe, they would find a way to stop you."

Before Kayla could say another word, Jessie was back; his face white and Kayla knew Nate had told him. She crossed her arms and watched as Jessie approached Eric. Her ears pricked up as Jessie whispered into Eric's ear and explained everything Kayla said to Nate.

With wide eyes, Eric turned to Kayla. "Is it true?"

"What?" Kayla spat, hoping beyond hope that something was lost in translation. But, she knew by the glare in Eric's eyes and Jessie's paleness, that Nate had shared her confession.

"You know what, don't play coy. Nate told Jessie everything."

"Did he now?" The small piece of Kayla's heart that held onto Nate broke off and shattered at her feet. Kayla sucked in a deep breath as Eric stepped back.

"You have no right to challenge my son," Eric started as Jessie reached out and grabbed Eric's shoulder. "But we will let the tribe decide who will lead them. Jessie."

Jessie rushed Kayla and swooped her up onto his shoulder. Kayla clawed and screamed as Eric and Jessie brought her back into town. With each kick and scream Kayla understood the pain that Naku had felt for her children. Just as Matoki's fate had been stripped from her, so Kayla's fate was also, as Eric and Jessie brought her back to the village.

Chapter 10

The moment Kayla's feet touched the ground; she raised her knee and gutted Jessie in the stomach. He dropped to the ground, as people began surrounding the stage. For a moment Kayla wondered how they had got there so quickly, but as she glanced at Eric she understood. Eric slipped a small black device into his pocket and crossed his arms.

The crowd around the stage grew and the moments ticked by. Kayla's nerves rattled as thoughts of being tied up again filled her mind. She wondered how many of them she could take down before they killed her. As she braced herself for a fight, Eric raised his hands causing the crowd to hush.

"It seems we have a challenger," Eric's voice boomed over the crowd and drifted out to the shops that lined the center. The crowd cheered and hissed as he spoke. Kayla scanned the audience looking for a weak link she could exploit. To her surprise, Nate's face was among the crowd. She glared at him as he looked up at her. His eyes were filled with apologies as Eric continued.

"The spirits have spoken to this girl," Eric mocked.

"Oh really? And what did they say?" A male voice boomed, demanding her to answer. Kayla's eyes shifted from Nate to find the man stepping forward. She gasped as she looked at him. Adam approached the stage and climbed up to stand beside Kayla.

"Well? I am curious, what did the spirits tell you that they haven't said to Eric?"

Kayla stared at Adam and sucked in a deep breath. As she sized him up, her eyes shifted to the dark woman standing behind him. Naku put her hand on Adam's shoulder and smiled. Kayla nodded as Naku spoke.

"Your stories are wrong. The history you know of this tribe is wrong. The gift you have to shift from animal to man was a curse the spirits put on this tribe."

The crowd laughed as Kayla spoke. The roaring laughter echoed in Kayla's ears. However, as Naku leaned in closer, Kayla's wicked smile grew.

"Holy shit," Adam gasped and his body shivered like the last leaf on a twig clinging to life in the dead of winter. Kayla's smile grew as she watched Naku blow into

Adam's ear. Although Adam saw nothing, Kayla noticed the blood draining from his face, turning him white.

"She is behind you Adam," Kayla laughed. "Naku knows the things you keep hidden. Do you want her to reveal those things to me? To the crowd?" Kayla raised her eyebrow accusingly as Adam shook his head.

"Enough of this," Eric demanded as he noticed Adam's allegiance shifting. "We will settle this the old way."

The crowd burst into cheers and several people raced to their shops to bring back chairs. Kayla's eyes scanned the crowd searching for any clues about what was coming. As her eyes found Nate, she gasped. His head was bowed as he turned and pushed his way through the crowd.

"Let him go," Naku said as Kayla's heart raced. Although she blamed Nate for this mess, she cared for him. Now he was leaving her to fend off the wolves alone.

"What is going on?" Kayla asked and her eyes shifted to Naku. The woman smiled as she vanished before Kayla.

"A spirit journey," Eric answered. His hot breath on Kayla's neck caused her to jump. She whipped her head around to glare at Adam who had regained some color in his face.

"Adam, attend to Kayla. Prep her for what is to come. I will do the same for Jessie. We will meet back here at nightfall."

Adam looped his arm around Kayla's and gestured for her to follow. Befuddled, Kayla allowed Adam to lead the way to the stairs and through the crowd. Only when they were alone in the furthest alley of town, did Adam suck in a deep breath. His eyes were wide with questions as he stared at Kayla. She glanced around the dirty alley wondering why they were there.

Only three doors lined the brick walls of the alleyway. Kayla paused at the last door waiting patiently as Adam paced the length of the area. Kayla tried to spy Nate in the opening, but he was nowhere to be seen. Kayla shook her head as hope faded from her.

"Never in all my years," Adam said, looking through Kayla as if she were glass. For a moment, Kayla wondered if he was talking to her at all.

"I knew they were around, you know," Adam's voice rose with excitement. "I knew they were listening. I just never thought that they were actually real you know?" Adam's eyes focused, and he stared right at Kayla. Unamused Kayla crossed her arms and waited.

"So what is this spirit walk all about?"

"Oh, right." Adam pulled keys from his pocket and unlocked the door. Kayla stepped into the dark room wondering if this would be her final resting place. Her heart drummed in her ears as her eyes adjusted to the dark.

"Okay so," Adam said and walking past her, he flicked on a switch. Kayla shielded her eyes as the room flooded with a blinding light. Long curtains draped down from the ceiling and crates filled the room. She took a hesitant step further into the room as Adam appeared with two chairs and sat them down in the middle of the room.

"A spirit journey is going to take you to the other side."

"The other side of what?" Kayla glared at him as Adam smiled.

"Life. You and Jessie are essentially going to leave your bodies and travel to the underworld."

"What the hell? No way. Not happening."

"Look, it's not a permanent thing. You get to come back."

"Says you. Have you ever done this?" Kayla crossed her arms as she stood next to the empty seat. Adam pressed his lips together and shook his head.

"No. But not because I didn't want to. It is more for leaders of the tribe to sort things out. The spirits guide the leaders of our tribe out of the obstacles and back to their body."

"Has anyone ever died?"

Adam didn't speak and his eyes shifted about the room dodging the question. Kayla nodded as she sat down in the chair as glared at him.

"It can happen," Adam broke. "If someone, who is only claiming to be a leader, goes to the other side, they won't come back."

"So that is why Eric wants this test. He thinks I don't have the spirits with me and that I will die in the challenge."

"Possibly. Or he thinks you will chicken out in which case, he wins."

"What do you think?" Kayla asked as she let her arms slump to her lap.

"After what you told me on stage, I have no doubt that Naku is with you. But what if Toko is with Jessie? That could cause some serious problems."

"Why?"

"Toko was the first man to shift. It is through his blood that we all can."

"Toko was not the first to shift. Naku's children shifted first. The twins. It was out of his rage that Toko shifted, before killing Naku."

Adam leaned back in his chair as Kayla told the story. His eye widened as he took in all she had to say. When Kayla was finished, Adam nodded, his mouth agape.

"That makes more sense. Naku was a healer. She could call on the spirits any time for help. She used her gift to ask them to help her daughter. But instead of picking one child, the spirits picked both." Adam rubbed his chin as he mulled over the information.

"I am going to have to write this down for future generations. If I was you, I would take this time to rest. The journey will drain you and if you come back, you will need your wits about you."

"I can't sleep."

"Try. At least rest, trust me on this, you are going to need it."

Adam rose from his seat and disappeared behind a closed door leaving Kayla to her thoughts. She glanced around looking for somewhere to rest her head.

"At least it's not a barn," she mumbled as she pushed crates and boxes aside and lay down on the cold stone floor.

Her mind raced with all that was coming and Nate's face came back to haunt her. She rolled over and closed her eyes trying to push him out of her mind. However, with each try, Nate only grew in more detail, until even his scent filled her nose.

"I love you," Kayla huffed as she squeezed her eyes tight and waited for nightfall.

Chapter 11

"It's time."

Kayla's eyes popped open and she jolted up from the floor. Her heart raced in her chest as her eyes scanned the room. Adam stepped back with his hands up as Kayla made the connection. She lowered her arms and relaxed her fists. Adam helped her to her feet.

"Sorry," Kayla stretched the sleep from her body as orange light flickered from the windows.

"It's okay. I figured once you started snoring, I should wake you cautiously."

"I don't snore."

"Yeah, you do." Adam laughed. He pulled out his phone to show Kayla the video he had recorded. On the small screen Kayla watched herself breathing deeply before muttering. Then a loud snore ripped through the room. Kayla flinched as she pulled away from the phone.

"Okay, fine. I snore."

"Like logs. But hey, at least you got some sleep right?"

"Sure." But Kayla knew her rest was far from peaceful.

"Well, let's get this over with shall we?"

"Adam," Kayla paused at the door as her nerves rattled. "If I don't see you again, can you tell Nate that I love him?"

"You will be fine," Adam said placing his hand on Kayla's shoulder. "You can tell him yourself later."

"But in case I don't come back." Kayla's eyes glanced to her feet as she waited for Adam's response.

"Of course. But you have this in the bag. Now let's go show them who the true Alpha is."

She nodded as Adam pushed through the door. The warm night air caressed Kayla's already blazing skin. She sucked in a deep breath as she stepped out into the alley way. Cheers and boos filled the small square and Adam pushed people aside, clearing a path for Kayla.

"Ah, there she is," Eric's voice boomed over the hissing crowd as she climbed the stairs to the stage.

"Any last words?" Eric grinned as Kayla took her place beside Jessie. She shook her head and Eric handed her a small glass. Kayla put the glass to her nose as Eric gave Jessie one too. For a moment Kayla's stomach twisted. The aroma coming from the small container was vile and revolting. There was no way she was going to be able to drink it without it coming back up.

"If you will." Eric lowered his hands to show the pile of blankets and pillows ready for them to rest on. With a cocky glare in his eyes, Jessie dropped down first. Kayla watched as Jessie raised the glass to the sky and downed the contents. The crowd cheered and clapped as Jessie's eyes drifted shut and he fell against the pillows, out cold.

"Your turn," Eric sneered as Kayla sat down near the pillows. She glanced at the reddish liquid in the glass before scanning the crowd. Adam shot her two thumbs up and a big smile as she put the glass to her lips and swallowed the contents.

Her vision blurred straight away, and her toes tingled. A sensation of pins and needles coursed throughout her body. The moment her head hit the pillow, she lost all feeling. Blackness surrounded her. Only the distant drumming of her heart filled the void.

"Hello?" Kayla's voice echoed into the abyss as a bright light no bigger than a pin hole shot through the veil of night. Kayla hesitated to move. Although she couldn't see anything around her, a sense of dread consumed her. She swallowed the lump of fear in her throat and moved.

Kayla's eyes widened as the distant light in that single step filled her consciousness. She lifted her hand up to shield her eyes as they focused on her new surroundings.

"Well, look who finally decided to get up." A dark shadow eclipsed the light allowing Kayla time to adjust. The longer she stood there, the more details came in to view. Her mouth dropped open as she saw Nate walking over to her to hand her a glass of clear liquid.

"Nate?"

"What's up sleepy head? Did you rest well?"

"What are you talking about? Where am I?"

"Seriously? How much did you drink last night?"

"Nothing," Kayla answered as her head began to pound with the beat of her heart. Each throb shocked her system causing her body to sway. She reached out and Nate grabbed her.

"Right. Come on, let's get you comfortable."

Nate helped Kayla to the couch in the living room and Kayla sank down into the comfy cushions. She glanced up at Nate with confusion stretched across her face.

"What happened?"

Nate's laughter filled the room. "We were celebrating, don't you remember?" Nate's fingers drifted over Kayla's arm and lifted her hand up to her face. There on her left hand a stunning ring of sapphire sparkled in the light. Kayla tried to focus.

"No, this isn't right. You didn't give me a ring."

"Clearly I did. And you said yes, so you can't take that back now." Kayla shook her head as she forced the memory to come back.

"Well, if you don't remember that, maybe this might jog your memory." Nate leaned down and kissed Kayla's neck. His tender lips pressed against her flesh causing her body to jerk.

"What's wrong? Ticklish?" Nate mumbled as he moved from her neck to her collar bone. Kayla closed her eyes allowing Nate to caress her tenderly.

"I'm sorry you know." Kayla mumbled as Nate's fingers slipped over her body undoing the buttons to her blouse.

"You can be stubborn, but I forgive you." Kayla sighed as his hot breath hit her ear and his hand slipped under the fabric of her shirt. Inch by inch, Nate's hand glided over her skin until it reached her breast. With two fingers, Nate pinched Kayla's nipple, and he bit her earlobe sending the perfect mix of pleasure and pain.

"I want you," Nate moaned in a deep voice. Kayla's heart skipped a beat as Nate released her nipple and drifted down over her stomach, stopping at her waist.

"I want all of you. Every inch of you and the wolf."

"Nate," Kayla struggled to speak as her breathing became erratic.

"Kayla."

"Wait," Kayla panted and her eyes sprang open. She scrambled to the other end of the couch as Nate dropped his head.

"What? Don't you want this?" his voice grew angry as he stared at her. Kayla shook her head looking wildly about the room. Nothing about it reminded her of home. Kayla sucked in a deep breath only to wrinkle her nose.

"What is this place?" Kayla glared at Nate as he rose from the floor and sat on the couch.

"Our home silly."

"We don't live together," Kayla said as Nate inched closer to her with lust in his eyes.

"Yes we do. Your clothes are here aren't they?" Kayla glanced around trying to find a room, a door, anything but nothing was right. She slipped off the couch keeping it between her and Nate.

"Where are we?"

"Your home."

"This is not my home."

"Honey, it pains me to think you don't want this." Nate's tenderness vanished as he smiled at her.

"You're not real."

"I am as real as you are." Nate lunged over the couch wrapping his arms around Kayla. Together they dropped to the floor as Nate forced his body down on her.

With both hands he grabbed Kayla's wrists and yanked her hands over her head.

"Let go of me." Kayla ordered glaring right into Nate's eyes. Nate cocked his head as if hearing something in the distance. Kayla's heart sank as she realized her words held no weight.

"Oh, somebody is in a bad mood."

"So help me. I don't want to hurt you."

"Yes you do. Come on, do your worst." Nate leaned down and hissed into Kayla's ear. She jumped as his tongue lapped over her lobe. A cold chill froze her and she glared at him with hate.

"You're not my Nate. He would never do this."

"Or maybe I would. How well do you know me, really?"

"If you love me, you would let me go," Kayla switched tactics as she tried to wiggle herself free from his grasp.

"But I don't love you." Nate's eyes narrowed on Kayla as he spoke. The gray of his eyes faded into black as Kayla stared at him.

"That's because you aren't Nate." Kayla didn't give the imposter time to react. She let the heat from the center of her being fill her body. The flames licked her flesh allowing her to shift from woman to the wolf. The moment she was free, Kayla lunged at the man in the room.

With her mouth wide, Kayla clenched her razor-sharp teeth around his neck and stopped just shy of biting his head off.

Chapter 12

The moment her teeth clamped down, the man was gone. Kayla stumbled forward, before turning about to find him. But, like the house, he was no longer in sight.

She turned herself around in circles only to see a wooden bridge leading out into the white light. She scanned the area studying each path.

"Think Kayla, you have to pick one," she said as she turned around again. "Make a choice."

She sucked in a deep breath and raced down the path to her right. Her nails clicked against the wood as she ran. The moment the clicking stopped, Kayla paused.

"Well done," Naku said with a smile on her face. The moment she saw Naku, Kayla let the cool air around her soothe the fire within her. With the flames extinguished, Kayla returned to her human form.

"What was that all about?"

"You had to face the wolf. Being what you are requires the balance of both worlds. You have to know when to let the wolf out and when to tame it."

"Why Nate?"

"The wolf takes many forms, Nate was merely one. Now come, there is more to do."

Kayla glanced around. Trees that were taller than the sky sprang forth from the ground blocking out the light of the sun. Kayla sighed as she followed Naku deeper into the forest.

"What is that?" Kayla stopped as an orange light rose between the thick trunks of the trees.

"The other one. The imposter."

"What?" Kayla didn't wait for further explanation. She took off running towards the fire. The moment the heat of the flames scorched her skin, she stopped.

"Jessie!"

Jessie glanced over to Kayla as the flames licked every inch of him. His face was contorted with pain and the fire was holding him prisoner. As she watched in horror, he reached out for her, unable to touch her.

"I wouldn't do that if I was you," Naku said as she walked out of the forest and joined Kayla.

"Why is he like that?"

"He does not belong here. He is not the Alpha of this tribe. But still he took the challenge and failed."

"I can't leave him here." Kayla reached out her hand and pushed through the flames. Jessie clasped his fingers around her wrist as Kayla pulled him out of his torture.

Jessie dropped to Kayla's feet choking and gasping for air. Naku glared at Kayla as she dropped to help him.

"Take deep breaths, you'll be fine."

"How?" Jessie choked, fighting for every bit of clean air his lungs could take.

"How do you think intruder? She is the rightful heir and Alpha. Show your allegiance to her or remain here forever." Naku's face darkened as she spoke causing the surrounding light to be snuffed out. Kayla grabbed Jessie around the shoulders and shook her head.

"You don't have to do this," Kayla pleaded as Jessie stared at her in wonder.

"No, but I want to. Naku is right, you were right. I am an imposter. I should have never challenged you."

"You didn't. Eric did and sent you to deal with me. Only he thought I would be the one in trouble not you."

"My father did this to me?" The words slipped off Jessie's lips as the truth sank in. He coughed and gagged as he nodded.

"I can't leave can I? Only the Alpha can pass through this place unharmed and I am not that man."

"I am not going to leave you here." Kayla glared at Naku, daring her to stop her from claiming Jessie. Naku smiled and the light returned to the forest.

"Go then, the both of you," Naku said and she stepped away from them. Kayla scooped one arm under Jessie's waist and draped his arm over her shoulder to help him to his feet.

"You have already done your part by sharing my story," Naku said as her body faded. "Now live the life my child was denied."

As Naku drifted away, Kayla noticed the same small bridge she had crossed moments ago. She hoisted Jessie closer to her and smiled.

"That's our ticket home. You ready?"

"I am sorry for everything."

"Don't worry about it."

"No," Jessie glanced up at her with awe and respect. He tried to stiffen his shoulders, but the pain shocked him.

"You deserve my brother. I see that now."

"I will remember you said that when we get back. Now let's get out of this fun house of horrors."

Kayla and Jessie moved slowly through the clearing towards the bridge. As soon as her foot dropped down on the wooden platform, she shot up sucking in a deep breath. With wild eyes, she glanced about. The bystanders gasped, and the village filled with murmurs.

"Jessie?" Eric's voice rose above the crowd as he dropped to his son's side.

"Jessie?" Kayla scrambled to Jessie's side and pressed her head to his chest.

"I don't understand. I had him with me when we crossed over. He should wake up."

"What did you do to him?" Eric shouted as he shoved Kayla off his son.

"I didn't do this to him. You did. You knew the consequences of the journey. You sent him to die in your place because you don't have the balls to stand up to me yourself."

A howl ripped through Eric's throat, as the old man shifted into his massive wolf form. Kayla didn't need to shift. She stared at the old man with trembling legs.

"I am the rightful Alpha of this tribe and you will stand down." Kayla's words were laced with orders. Eric's knees buckled as he tried to lunge at her. The weight of Eric in wolf form crashed against Jessie's chest. Jessie jolted up sucking in a deep breath as he felt his father on top of him.

"Dad?" he huffed as he tried to push his father off him. Kayla shook her head as Eric moved slowly off his son. The sight of Jessie calmed him and Eric shifted back to human form.

"I am sorry," Eric dropped to his knees next to Jessie. "I thought you would..."

"I know dad. But now we know better don't we?" Jessie glanced up to Kayla and nodded. Kayla gave a faint smile before turning to the stunned crowd.

"I never asked to be your Alpha. I didn't want the position – heck, I barely know a quarter of you." Kayla's eyes drifted to Alice, who waited for her husband to return. Alice smiled wide as she wiped away the tears streaming from her eyes.

"That is why I think it would be best for everyone if Jessie remains the leader of this tribe." Kayla extended her hand down to Jessie and pulled him to his feet. Eric's mouth dropped as Jessie wrapped his arms around Kayla in unity.

The crowd cheered as Kayla pulled away from Jessie and kissed him on the cheek. "I won't forget what you did for me," Jessie whispered.

"I hope not."

Alice bolted to the stage and wrapped her arms around Jessie's neck pulling him closer to her. Jessie laughed as Alice kissed every inch of his face.

"Don't ever scare me like that again got it?" Alice scolded. Kayla scanned the crowd before returning her gaze to Alice and Jessie.

"He's not here." Alice said and the joy left her face. Kayla nodded and her heart sank. Although she had hoped to find Nate there, she knew he wouldn't come. Not after what she had done to him.

"You might find him down by the creek. He likes to go there sometimes to hunt," Jessie said as he turned to Eric. Kayla's gaze drifted to Eric who remained kneeling on the stage. Eric nodded as he looked up to Kayla.

"Go. As Alpha you have the right to choose your mate. I know my son loves you."

"Believe it or not, I love him too."

"Well, what are you doing here? Go get him!" Alice giggled. Kayla's sober expression turned to hope as she jumped off the stage. The crowd parted as she raced towards the forest.

Chapter 13

The forest opened up before her as she sprinted towards the river. Every fiber of her being cried out and she prayed that she wasn't too late for redemption. When she reached the edge of the water she stopped and turned. No matter which direction she faced, she couldn't pick up Nate's scent.

"Dammit, where are you?" Kayla panted and she knelt over, trying to regain her breathing. She closed her eyes allowing the rushing flow of water fill her ears. Each twig that snapped, every branch that moaned with the wind, Kayla heard, but no sign of claws scrapping against the earth. Kayla stood up and sighed.

"Naku!" Kayla's voice drifted into the night. "I know you can hear me. Tell me where he is."

"Where do you think he is?" Naku answered. Kayla spun on her heels and she saw Naku turn and point.

"Thank you." Kayla called back as she mustered all her strength to keep going.

"Don't think for an instant that you can't summon me whenever you want." Naku scolded after Kayla as a smile played on her lips. Kayla dismissed Naku as she forced herself to keep moving.

Through the dead of night Kayla found the edge of the road. The slick black pavement stretched on for miles. There at the edge of the forest Kayla found the musky scent she loved so much.

"Please be there," Kayla said as she looked both ways before crossing the road. As the forest grew thinner, Kayla found herself in the clearing. Hidden in the high grass, a gray wolf perked his head up.

"Nate?" Kayla moved closer trying to not to spook him. She knew beyond a shadow of doubt that Nate would never hurt her. But she didn't know how long he had been in wolf form. Nate's eyes widened as Kayla came closer. A smile erased her concern, as Nate shifted back into his human form.

"You're alive!" Nate raced to Kayla with arms out ready to scoop her up.

"I'm so sorry," Nate gasped between his kisses. "If I had known that my dad would challenge you that way..."

Their lips crashed together with a hunger that consumed them. As Nate's hands curled around Kayla's body, she knew she was home. It didn't matter if they were in the forest or in the tiny one-bedroom house, Kayla didn't want to be anywhere but next to him.

"It's okay," Kayla sighed as she squeezed him tighter. Suddenly, Nate dropped his arms and cupped his hands around Kayla's face. His sober stare sent chills through her. Her heart skipped as she waited for the other shoe to drop.

"If you are here, then Jessie..." Nate's voice trailed off and his gaze drifted towards the trees behind Kayla. She placed her hands on Nate's and smiled.

"He's fine. If you want, you can go and see him."

"But how? The spirits would only accept the true Alpha."

"And I told the spirits to shove it." Kayla laughed as Nate stared at her, and then a spark in his eyes replaced the sorrow.

"I'm not Alpha though. I gave the position to Jessie. He knows how to rule this village better than I do. Besides, I'm not sure having that authority is best. The commands I give take away people's will." Kayla dropped her gaze and turned from Nate. Her heart filled with regret as she turned her back to him.

"Nate, I am so sorry for commanding you as I did. I am sorry for using that against you."

"No." Nate grabbed Kayla's hand and twisted her around to face him.

"You don't get to apologize for that. I crossed the line, and you defended yourself."

"I am still sorry."

"I know and I forgive you." Nate moved in taking Kayla by the waist. "So what happens now?"

Kayla smiled as she wrapped her arms around his neck and planted a kiss on his lips. "I don't know. How about we start with roommates and see what happens?"

Nate's eyes widened as his lips parted into a huge smile that filled Kayla's heart.

"Really? You mean it?"

"I love you Nate. I was afraid to say it before, but I'm not anymore."

"What changed your mind?"

Kayla's mind drifted back to the spirit world for a brief moment. The trials she had faced had brought her face-to-face with herself. She turned and stared deep into Nate's eyes.

"You did." Kayla curled her legs around Nate's body forcing him to hold her. She smiled as she kissed him under the pale moonlight.

"Maybe we can take this someplace else?" Nate asked pulling away for just a moment. Kayla giggled as set her feet back down.

"Let's go home."

Epilogue

Jessie stared at himself in the mirror, studying his face as the water dripped off his chin. The horrors of the underworld rushed back into his mind and he tried to steady his nerves.

"Hey Hon, you okay?" Alice's tiny voice called from the other side of the door and her light knocking pulled him back to reality.

"I don't know." Jessie said as Naku glared at him through the reflection. Jessie spun around, his heart pounding in his chest and the dark figure approached him.

"We have some unfinished business, you and I." Naku reached out and touched Jessie on the shoulder. He opened his mouth wide to release the scream but only silence filled the room.

"Don't worry, you are not the one I am after," she said as the light of the bathroom faded into darkness.

END

The Fate of the Alpha
The Wolf Pack Bloodlines Series

Amelia Wilson

Table of Contents:

Prologue

Chapter 1

Chapter 2

Chapter 3

Chapter 4

Chapter 5

Chapter 6

Chapter 7

Chapter 8

Chapter 9

Chapter 10

Chapter 11

Epilogue

Prologue

"Honey?"

Alice's voice strained as she turned her head towards the stairs. Her ears perked up, waiting for Jessie's answer. The flow of water from the upstairs shower filled her ears and she waited. Thunder rumbled outside as she shifted her weight to get a better view of the staircase. She knew Jessie would be out of the shower soon: but still, something ached in her bones making her restless.

The silence that filled the house was haunting, as Jessie cut off the water. She turned the television down trying to hear him as her uneasiness grew.

"Jessie!" She cried out louder, hoping that her voice would carry up into the bathroom. She paused and held her breath while she waited for his response. All that filled her ears was the hollowness of silence.

"Honey, you are going to miss the beginning," she grumbled as she set the popcorn down on the table and stood up from the sofa.

"I'm serious. I will start the show without you."

The wooden floor creaked as she moved around the furniture and headed towards the stairs. Her body stiffened and she called once again, only to get back more of the same eerie silence as before. She shifted her eyes to the television, where the screen remained paused. Every hair on the back of her head stood on end while she waited for him to answer. Dread filled her and her heart drummed faster and faster.

"Jessie?"

Alice started up the stairs, as the hair on the back of her neck prickled. Each wooden plank on the risers bent under her weight as she climbed up towards the bedroom. A crack of lightening followed by the roaring thunder set her on edge. Despite her excellent night vision, the shadows seemed darker. She sucked in a deep breath when she reached the last step and she paused. Her ears twitched at the slightest sound. Within the deepest part of her being, she hoped to hear something from the upstairs bathroom.

"Jessie?" she called again and her voice cracked from the stress. She moved carefully towards the bedroom, flipping on the hall light as she moved. Even the light that flooded the hallway seemed dimmer than before.

"It's just the storm," she mumbled to herself trying to hold back her fear. She knew that Jessie was here; that she wasn't alone, yet the shadows followed her as she made her way to the bedroom door.

With a trembling hand, she reached out and twisted the knob of the bedroom door. The creaking of the hinges startled her and she carefully pushed it open. More shadows greeted her as she walked into the room. The only source of light came from under the bathroom door. Yellow light flooded the carpet and spread out like fingers clawing into the darkness.

She sucked in a deep breath and stepped closer to the bathroom door. In her head, voices screamed at her to run. Every instinct begged her to go, but she couldn't bring herself to listen to them. After all, Jessie was on the other side of the closed door.

"No more scary movies for you," Alice told herself as she raised her wary hand. She rapped lightly and quickly on the wooden frame. The sound drummed in her ears like the rolling thunder outside. She stood back and listened. Branches from the trees outside scrapped against the window. The sound was like nails on a chalkboard and sent her into a panic. Her eyes darted to the shadows in the room as she flipped on the light, banishing the shadows to the corners of the room.

"Seriously Jessie, you are starting to freak me out." Her voice wavered and she pressed her ear up to the door, waiting for him to say something.

Behind the door, the young man panted, trying to catch his breath. Each pull of fresh air into his lungs burned as if he had just finished a marathon. He grabbed the basin and held onto it as the hot air from the shower filled his lungs. Panic filled him and he tried, once again, to answer Alice. He opened his mouth wide trying to force the words to come out and to tell her to run. But not even a whimper escaped his lips.

Each heart beat seemed to stretch on for an eternity as he tried to move. Jessie's heart pounded in his rib cage and echoed in his ears like thunder ripping through a cavern. Not even the raging storm outside could break through his fear as he stared at the dark, cloaked figure before him.

"Alice, RUN!" he tried to scream as the figure remained still before him.

Only the white of its eyes peered back at him, piercing the darkness that shrouded it. He sucked in a shallow breath. The eyes remained locked on him, keeping him prisoner in his own bathroom. The longer Jessie stared at the figure, the more deeply it peered into his soul, stealing the very life from him. For a brief moment he wondered if he was being pulled back into the spirit world and that this figure had returned to collect him.

After all, he had heard those tales of those that enter the spirit world uninvited. Had it not have been for Kayla, he would still be there, now, burning in an eternal flame. However, as his fingers gripped the basin of the sink more tightly, he knew precisely where he was. His surroundings hadn't changed, only his company.

"This has to be dream," he thought as he tried to blink away the image. But even that idea was short lived because the figure drew closer and still he hadn't awakened from the nightmare. The figure's wicked smile sent chills racing down his bare back and his body trembled, unable to move. No matter how much he fought for control over himself, he knew he was losing.

"Not happening," he mumbled the mantra inside his head as the figure stepped closer. Fear stole the very breath from him as he tried to call out for Alice once again. He could smell her sweet honeysuckle perfume on the other side of the door. He knew that she was close enough to pull him from this trance if only he could tell her what to do. But Alice wouldn't be able to stop the figure and Jessie knew it.

"Get Kayla," Jessie wanted to scream. "Get her here now! Please, Alice, someone, help me!" His tongue however, did not do as he commanded and his voice broke over each syllable, making the plea more of a gurgle of unintelligent noises.

"This won't hurt a bit," the figure cackled and its laugh filled the bathroom. Jessie braced himself for the attack. He sucked in a deep breath wondering if it would be his last.

"Jessie? Hurry up, will ya? The show is on and you are really scaring me."

Alice's hand trembled as she twisted the knob to the bathroom door. Slowly light poured out as she cracked the door. Relief washed over her when she spied Jessie standing at the sink with his head down. The mere sight of him washed away the fear that had held her hostage. But, by the look of him, she knew something was off. He didn't turn to greet her. He didn't say anything. He just stood there, and questions filled Alice's mind.

"If you don't want to watch a movie, we can always do something else," Alice forced a giggle, trying to ease the tension in the room. She raised her hand to brush her fingers down Jessie's spine. Her light touch on his shoulder caused him to jump and his eyes popped open. Whipping his head around, Jessie growled at her as if she were the intruder. Alice pulled her hand back and glared at him and the fear that she had tried so desperately to shut away stung her.

"Jessie? What's wrong?" She stared up at him studying him. The light in his eyes shifted and Alice's gaze grew concerned.

"Are you okay?" Alice asked, circling around him. Her eyes were trained on his face as she tried to find any sign of an injury. She sat down carefully on the edge of the tub and curled herself up. Her eyes filled with wonder and confusion. She had been with Jessie for so many years, she wondered if he had finally had enough of her. She waited for the confession. She could see the turmoil in his face as he struggled to speak but still, he remained silent.

"Just say it already," Alice demanded as her heartbeat slammed into her chest. She wiped her hands on her jeans and waited.

Jessie glanced at her and tossed his head about causing water to sprinkle over Alice. She lifted her hand to block the spray, as Jessie settled and stared at her briefly before turning. Without a sound or even a whimper he tore off the towel around his waist and let the animal loose.

"Hey, not in the house!" Alice scolded as she followed the brown wolf out of the bathroom and into their bedroom. She paused at the door and used it as a shield as the wolf strolled out the bedroom down the stairs.

"Come on Jessie, this isn't funny." Shock and dread rattled Alice as she stalked the creature from the top floor. She was filled with bewilderment as she watched the massive animal stumble around the furniture. It let out a growl and then it lunged for the front door ripping the screen from the hinges.

Alice raced down the stairs in a panic, attempting to follow him, but she was too late. By the time she had stepped outside and shifted, his scent had vanished. All that remained was the lingering wet fragrance of grass and gasoline, as vehicles drove down the street. In the distance she spotted a dark shadow moving too swiftly to be a wolf. But, it too vanished with the crack of lightening above her.

"Jessie?!" Alice's cry faded from his ears as he pushed himself further and faster than ever before. The need to hunt overpowered him, as he dodged oncoming vehicles and raced to get to the woods.

With his nails scrapping into the asphalt, Jessie skidded to a stop. On the wind a familiar scent caught his attention. Slowly and steadily he stalked through the night, following the brief whiffs of the scent that caused the hairs on the back of his neck to rise. Through the rain and wind, Jessie hunted down the musky aroma until he found himself at the window of a house.

"That's the one," he thought as he glared in through the window. A growl ripped through his body as he stared at the withered man inside. With his heart racing and muscles twitching, he waited for his moment. There was only one thing on his mind, one thing that would make the craving go away. Jessie licked his snout and watched as animal desires and cravings overpowered his human self.

Chapter 1

The hard tapping of the rain against the window irritated Kayla. She tossed in her bed, as the consistent drumming against the glass rattled her nerves. She reached over her head and pulled the pillow over it to drown out the noise, but still the drumming broke through making it impossible for her to sleep.

She threw the pillow away from her and turned her head. Beside her, Nate rested soundly and his snores filled the room. She wrapped her arm around Nate's slumbering body, trying to drown the sound by listening to the steady rhythm of his heart. Although the sound was comforting, it wasn't enough to calm her. Nate's body heat was too much for her and she knew she would have to move sooner or later.

"No sleep for you tonight," she mumbled as she watched, jealously, how easily Nate could sleep through anything.

Kayla tried to focus on something else to get her body and mind to be still. Her eyes lingered on her arm draped over Nate's body. She watched her arm rise and fall to his breathing. Lightning shattered the dark room, illuminating her surroundings for a brief moment before the darkness engulfed everything once again. Nate shifted as Kayla scooted herself closer to him trying to bury her head in his chest.

Still, the hammering of the rain unsettled her. Her heart drummed in her chest as her eyes darted about the room. Only one thing would get her to sleep tonight, only one thing would calm her enough to get some sleep. A smile played at the corner of her lips as her eyes shifted to Nate's peaceful face. Her wicked grin of temptation grew to full-blown smile as she slipped her hand slowly under the sheets. Inch by inch she moved further down, allowing her fingers to run freely over his smooth skin.

Nate mumbled as Kayla drifted her fingers over his inner thigh until she found her mark. Carefully, she cupped her hand around his groin. The warmth of her embrace caused Nate to stir. Kayla tried not to giggle as his cock twitched and jerked, as it awoke.

"Please," Nate whispered in his sleep shifting his body closer to her. She stifled her laugh trying not to break into Nate's dream. She wanted to hear his darkest thoughts and play with his deepest desires.

As her fingers drifted over his soft shaft and breached the crown, his cock grew under her fingertips. With each breath he pulled in, her passion grew. Kayla's fingertips drifted over his skin and raced around his inner thighs as if her fingers were miniature figure skaters dancing on ice. Her eyes remained locked on his movements and then she curled her fingers around the base of his shaft and pumped her hand.

Excitement filled her as she studied him. With every fluid push of her hand Nate's body responded. His breathing became erratic, as moisture pooled in her panties. For a moment Kayla wondered if now would be the right time to take what she wanted. She steadied herself on her elbow while she stripped the sheets from their bodies.

"More," he huffed as his body shifted and twitched. Kayla pressed her face to his chest trying to quiet her amusement.

"My love. Please, do what you want to me," Nate whispered. Kayla's ears perked up as she heard him speak. For a second she wondered if he had woken. The lightening crashed outside illuminating the room once again and she exhaled. With wide eyes, she stared at Nate wondering if her antics had woken him. She waited and watched for any signs of waking, but after a few moments it was clear he was still sound asleep.

Kayla shifted herself up to rest on her elbow trying to keep most of her weight off Nate as she opened her mouth wide. She wondered how pissed he would be if she did everything she wanted to do while he was still asleep. A ping of regret stabbed her, but was quickly diminished as Nate's hand fell on top of hers. Together, hand in hand, they stroked and pumped his cock causing it to drip.

She ran her thumb over the crown of his cock spreading the small amounts of fluid that leaked from his tip. Her body ached for his, ached for attention. She pressed herself against him. Her nipples tingled as she leaned closer. Nate's cock throbbed in her hand as she squeezed him.

"Yes," Nate pleaded as Kayla wrapped her lips around his head and consumed him. She closed her eyes allowing her sense of touch to fill every nerve. As her tongue rolled his hard penis in her mouth, she squeezed his shaft and dropped her hand.

With her little finger, she traced the veins of his sack, as he throbbed in her throat. Nate's hips jerked forcing Kayla to take more than she had expected. With quick reflexes, she pulled back and popped his dick from her mouth. She sat up abruptly as she swallowed hard, forcing her spit to sooth the irritation in the back of her throat. Her eyes shifted to him.

The low growl coming from Nate's chest assured her he was still sound asleep. Kayla scooted back down to resume her position. She grabbed Nate's shaft and pushed his crown into her tight lips. With her hand firmly in place, she managed to take in only what she wanted, despite Nate's constant hip jerking and thrusting upward. As her saliva coated the head, she rose up moving carefully over his body until she faced his feet. With her hand firmly stroking Nate's shaft, she positioned it between her legs. Every fiber of her body screamed as she eased down allowing her body to melt over his.

"What the-?" Nate's voice was no longer calm and peaceful. Kayla's smile grew as she rocked her hips forcing the tip of his cock to touch her inner walls. Kayla squeezed her muscles around Nate's cock as she rocked back and forth. Nate gasped for air and his hand flew to her hips.

"I thought-," he panted as Kayla's hand drifted over her body. "-dreaming." Nate finally finished as she forced her body down in quick movements before shifting her hips to roll over his.

"Then it was a good dream?"

"You were... I was... Yes," Nate cooed as she pumped harder forcing the springs of the mattress to quake beneath their weight. Kayla pulled Nate out of her and laughed as he sighed.

"Where do you think you are going?" Nate asked scrambling to keep his hold on Kayla's body. His cock twitched from excitement as Kayla eased herself off the bed and stood at the edge with her hands on her hips.

"You can't just go for the good stuff," Kayla scolded.

"Oh really?" Nate shook his head as his arms stretched out for her. She smiled as she stepped back as his fingers grazed over her bare skin.

"See here," Nate huffed bolting from the bed. In an instant, Nate had his arms around Kayla's bare body. He lowered his body as he opened his mouth. She let out a sigh as Nate's tongue circled around her hardened nipple.

Despite the way Nate's tongue tickled her, Kayla allowed Nate's hands to roam her naked body. He pulled Kayla to him forcing her to stay skin to skin as his hands ventured south and cupped her ass.

"You're mine," Nate growled as Kayla tried to get away from the big bad wolf. She shook her head and tried to wiggle and squirm her way out of his grasp.

"So you say," Kayla cooed as Nate's left hand moved her over her hips, until his hand cupped her crotch.

"I do say. Every inch of you," Nate pulled back to stare Kayla in the eyes. His soft eyes bore into her as flashes of light filled the room. Kayla sucked in a sharp breath as Nate pushed two fingers past Kayla's pussy lips and dove into her body.

She arched her back as Nate opened his mouth to receive her perky breasts once more. Before she could wrap her head around the pressure of Nate's fingers, he pulled them out and rubbed her juices around her clit. "It's mine."

"Then fuck me like you mean it," Kayla said staring at Nate with the same fierce passion he had. "I don't want you to stop until I come. Do you understand?"

Kayla wrapped her fingers into Nate's hair yanking his head back as she spoke. There was no denying her demand for his attention. Nate's cock shot up as Kayla spoke. Her eyes shifted towards his member as she realized that he liked the dominatrix side of her.

"Yes," Nate hissed arching his head back to gaze up at Kayla. There was fierceness in her eyes that thrilled him. With a smile on his face, Nate pulled his hand away from Kayla's body. He shook his head as much as he could while it was restrained, until Kayla released him. She didn't hesitate, but climbed over the edge of the king size bed and waited for him.

Nate grabbed her hips and Kayla glanced over her shoulder. With one hand he snatched his cock and rammed it into her, hard. Her body rocked forward as their hips crashed against one another.

"Fuck," Kayla grunted as Nate pounded the air out of her. Each ram forced Kayla's body further up onto the bed. Only Nate's grip held her firmly in place.

"Like that? Is that how you want it tonight?" Nate huffed as Kayla's juices flowed over his shaft making it slippery.

"Harder," Kayla cried out as the thunder rumbled the windows. For all Kayla knew a hurricane was coming down around them. But her mind was elsewhere. She dove her head down into the mattress as she took all that Nate had to offer.

Each pump of his body, Kayla's body stretched. She moaned into the sheets as Nate's balls slapped against her ass. Nate's fingers dug into her sides as he growled and huffed.

"More," Kayla pleaded as Nate paused. She glanced over her shoulder waiting. As Nate pulled in air, he shook his head and held up a finger.

"Unacceptable." Kayla pulled her body away from Nate forcing his cock to slip out of her. She spun around and dropped to his side. A smile curled up at the corner of her lips as she saw his cock throbbing with anticipation. Leaning down, she wrapped her fingers around his shaft and drew her body closer to his. Her lips parted and she stuck out her tongue. The tip of her tongue licked over the edge of Nate's head. She pushed the tender flesh into her tight lips, filling her mouth. With her tongue rolling over his head, she tasted her own sweet nectar. She sat up with a smile on her face.

"My turn."

"What?" Nate's eyes widened as Kayla wrapped her hands around Nate's neck pulling him down on her. She flipped him around and moved gracefully until she was on top. Before he could protest, Kayla was again was mounted on top and pushed her weight down on him.

Nate's cock rubbed her inner walls causing her to throw her head back in pleasure. With each push, his stomach muscles tickled her clit. Kayla wiggled her hips each time she rose before slamming back down on his hard rod.

"You are going to make me come, if you keep that up."

"Good. I want you to fill me up. I want to feel your come shooting into my body."

"Kayla?" Nate gasped as she moved faster. Her body tightened as the intensity swelled within her. If he didn't come soon, there was no doubt in her mind she would.

Without warning, Kayla's inner walls clamped around Nate's throbbing cock. She cried out as her juices flowed out of her and covered every bit of Nate's lower body. Nate's fingers squeezed around her hips and his body jerked up, nearly knocking Kayla off him.

"Fuck!" Nate cried out as Kayla panted. Little white dots filled her vision and her body trembled. She tried blinking them away as she fell to Nate's chest.

"What brought that on?" Nate asked between breaths. Kayla smiled as she squeezed him and pressed her lips to his chest.

"Are you complaining?"

"Absolutely not. It's just unexpected, that's all."

"Well, if this storm keeps up, expect it again."

"Is that what it was? Restlessness because of the storm?"

"Something like that." Kayla smiled as she leaned forward pressing her lips to his. As they kissed, Kayla slipped Nate's spent out cock from her body.

"No," Nate grumbled as the cold air flowed over his body part.

"Sorry, but I have to go use the bathroom, and you can't very well come with me." Kayla giggled as she slipped off Nate and sat up. She threw her legs over the edge of the bed and stood. The white dots flashed about her eyes again, and her head spun.

"You okay there?" Nate chuckled as Kayla tried to walk in a straight line to the bathroom.

"Fine," Kayla lied as her big toe collided with the edge of the bed. "Ouch."

"Need help?"

"No." Kayla huffed as she fumbled towards the bathroom and flicked on the light.

Kayla glanced at herself in the mirror. Her mouth dropped as her eyes adjusted to the light. A girl with wide eyes and wild hair stared back at her. Kayla shook her head and laughed as she tried to fix herself up. Just as she had tamed her hair, a distant rapping caught her attention.

"Nate? You okay?" Kayla called out as she reached for her nightgown that was hanging on the back of the bathroom door.

"Get dressed love, we have company."

Chapter 2

Kayla's eyes focused on the tiny drops of water falling like diamonds from Alice's hair. She shook her head and handed Alice a tissue as the girl wept.

"I don't know what happened. One minute we are about to watch a movie and the next he was gone."

"What do you mean gone? Like vanished into thin air?" Nate leaned in closer looking at the poor girl before shifting his eyes to Kayla. Kayla shrugged. A million possibilities filtered through Kayla's mind as Alice continued.

"Jessie went upstairs to take a shower, before watching a movie with me. I got everything set up. When I called for him, he didn't answer. So, I went upstairs." Alice sniffled as she wiped away the tears from her eyes.

"And then what? He was gone?"

"No." Alice shook her head trying to hold back the sobs. "He was there, but he wasn't. It was like he didn't even see me. He walked past me and shifted into his wolf form. He knows I hate it when he does that. But then he fumbled around down stairs knocking into the furniture like he didn't know where he was. The next thing I saw was him plowing through the screen door. I tried to go after him, but he was gone. I don't know where he is or what happened to him."

Nate glanced at Kayla as she moved in closer to Alice. Kayla put her arm around the poor girl and hugged her. Alice curled into Kayla and let out a fresh torrent of uncontrollable sobs.

"We'll find him," Kayla promised and her eyes caught Nate's.

"I'll track him down," Nate stood and pulled his shirt off. The sight of Nate's bare skin thrilled Kayla. Raw passion swelled in her mind and it drifted to their fun upstairs. Kayla shook her head forcing the thought from her mind. After all, Alice was in tears. Now was not the time for such things.

"Maybe I should go," Kayla mumbled. "Maybe the spirits can help me find him faster."

"I thought they abandoned you when you turned down the role of alpha." Nate whipped his head toward Kayla. His mouth dropped, as Kayla turned her attention to Alice.

"Well, they aren't as loud as before," Kayla confessed. "So, I guess they are still around."

"Oh, please Kayla. If they can help that would be great." Alice's head popped up as hope changed her expression. An undeniable need for reassurance filled Alice as she turned to Nate.

"Besides," Kayla huffed. "The moisture in the air will make it nearly impossible to sniff him out. His trail is probably washed away."

"So, what do you need from me?" Nate asked returning to the couch and sitting on the other side of Alice.

"Stay here, I am going to see if Naku answers. Maybe she can tell us where Jessie went."

Kayla rose from the couch and moved through the house. The squeaky springs moaned as she pulled open the screen door and stepped out into the night. The cool air whipped around her body as tiny drops filtered through her thin nightgown. Kayla glanced around the open space as she forced herself to concentrate. Although she had done this before, she didn't know if it would work with Jessie. The last time it was for her own desires, now she was tracking down someone for another. She wondered if she could, as she glanced up to the dark sky.

Lightning danced from one cloud to another and she grabbed on to the railing of the porch. She calmed her mind and pushed herself to think of nothing but Jessie. As his image grew stronger in her mind, she sucked in a deep breath and held it.

"Where is he?" she whispered to the night. The crystal clear image of Jessie vanished from her mind and Naku's deep-set eyes flashed before her eyes. Kayla stumbled back from the onslaught of the vision. She shook her head and forced herself to concentrate once again.

"Where is Jessie?" Kayla demanded this time and she laced her question with alpha undertones. An unsettling laughter filled her ears and the thunder clapped. The image of Naku filled her mind. A room grew brighter in Kayla's mind. Details became clearer the more she focused. Kayla saw Jessie, sitting on a leather couch in front of a roaring fire.

She exhaled as the image faded and then she closed her eyes and sighed. She turned her head and glanced over her shoulder towards the closed screen door. Behind the closed door, she knew a girl wept for her lost love. But although Kayla saw Jessie back at home, she knew something had happened to him; something that would be hard to explain.

Kayla stood up and turned around. She pulled open the screen door and stepped inside. Immediately Alice was on her feet. The hope in her eyes stabbed Kayla.

"Well? Did you find him?"

"He is home."

"Oh thank God. I need to get back there." Alice hugged Nate and moved swiftly for the front door. Kayla stretched out her arm restraining Alice from leaving.

"Kayla? What is going on? If Jessie is back home, then I should be there too."

"Alice, I think we all should go."

"Why? What's happened?"

"I don't know. But, I don't think you should be there alone with him, right now. I saw something strange and it wouldn't be right for us to let you walk into the wolf's den without some back up."

"Whatever happened I can handle it."

"We know," Nate said as he slipped his arms through his shirt and rose from the couch. "But it is better to be safe than sorry. Let me get my keys and we will go with you."

"I will meet you there. I can't very well go out like this," Kayla said glancing at her nightgown. The smile on Nate's lips pleased Kayla. She knew she could walk out of the house naked and Nate would be okay with it.

"Sure you can," Nate whispered as Kayla passed him. He lifted his hand up and brushed his fingertips over her arm. The electricity sparked every nerve in her body. She paused to let the sensation fill her.

"Just so you know," Kayla smiled. "I'm not done with you."

"I was hoping you would say that," Nate answered and he grabbed her arm and pulled her to him. As their lips parted, Alice cleared her throat.

"Guys, if you have other things to do, I can go alone."

Kayla pulled away from Nate. She wanted nothing more than to take him back to the bedroom. Her body was not yet satisfied, and she craved him more than ever. She shook her head forcing her animal nature to be still and pushed the desire away.

"No. Just give me just a second. I can't go out like this," Kayla smiled as her hand flowed over her nightgown. She winked at Nate before turning and moving towards the bedroom. As soon as she entered the room, she tore off her nightgown quickly and tossed it into the corner of the room. Her eyes scanned the floor searching for the last thing she had worn. She moved with purpose to the pile of clothes and threw on the first things her fingers touched. In a matter of minutes, Kayla walked back out of the room dressed and ready to go.

"Come on, let's go help Jessie," Kayla said and she glanced at Nate. Nate nodded and rose from the couch. Alice soon followed, wiping the tears from her eyes. Dread filled Kayla as she made her way towards the front door. From the vision she had had earlier, she knew that tonight was about to take a turn for the worst.

"Maybe it wasn't the storm after all," Nate whispered to Kayla. Kayla nodded as her nerves rattled. There was a reason Kayla was jittery tonight, but she still had no clue why.

Kayla followed Nate and Alice out the door. The rain spilled over the awning of the roof as Nate covered his head with his shirt to evade the torrential downpour. Alice was already soaked and she stepped out into the storm. A chill shook Kayla as she turned to lock up. She paused when she noticed Naku, standing in her living room, shaking her head with a wicked smile stretched across her face.

"You okay?" Nate asked pulling Kayla out of the vision. Kayla blinked and turned to stare at Nate.

"Sure," she lied and she joined Alice and Nate in the car. The engine roared to life and Kayla's stomach twisted as they pulled away from the house. She turned her attention to the darkness, and thoughts filled her mind. Whatever was about to come down, it was not going to be good and she knew it.

It didn't take long before the darkness was flooded by the lamps that lined the streets. Kayla knew everything that was going on inside every house they passed. She wondered if the pressure of being the alpha was what had caused Jessie to snap. After all, she had the spirits on her side. What were they doing to Jessie?

"The light is on!" Alice squealed as they pulled up to the house.

"Alice, be careful." Kayla warned as the engine died but Alice threw open the car door and booked it to the house.

"Nate," Kayla turned to Nate and a lump of fear choked her. She swallowed hard forcing it down. "This isn't going to be good."

Before Kayla could say another word, a scream broke the silence. Nate threw open the door and raced to the house. Kayla was on his heels as they pushed through the front door. Jessie lay on the couch in a fetal position, rocking.

"What the fuck?" Nate whimpered at the sight of his brother, who was also covered in blood.

Chapter 3

"Kayla get some towels, Alice, do you have any alcohol in this place?"

"Of course," Alice rushed to the kitchen and pulled a bottle from the top of the fridge. Kayla made her way to the bathroom and gathered as many towels as she could carry before making her way back down the stairs. Nate moved slowly towards Jessie, with his hands up, as the girls brought back the items.

"Here," Alice said handing Nate the bottle. Nate pushed the bottle in front of Jessie and Kayla walked into the kitchen and grabbed a pot from in the cabinet. Her eyes flickered to Nate and Jessie as she filled the pot up with warm water and brought it over to them.

"Jessie?" Nate's soothing voice tickled Kayla. From deep within her the desire to rip Nate away consumed her thoughts. She shook her head and pushed the fantasies aside.

"What is wrong with me?" Kayla wondered as Nate dipped a washcloth into the pot of water and squeezed out the excess. Little by little, Nate cleared the blood from Jessie's face.

"I did it. I didn't mean to. I couldn't stop. The..." Jessie mumbled as he rocked back and forth.

"Shhh," Alice cooed trying to keep him calm. "It's okay. Whatever happened, it will be okay."

"IT WON'T BE OKAY!" Jessie lunged at Alice with his teeth bared, ready to bite. Nate shoved him back on the couch and placed himself between Jessie and Alice.

"Just tell us what happened." Nate said as he wiped away more blood. "Or at least tell us if we need to call a doctor."

"It's not my blood," Jessie panted as he squeezed his eyes closed. Kayla stood at the back, watching as Nate tried to get Jessie to open up.

"Whose blood is it?" Nate asked as Alice stepped away in tears.

"His blood," Jessie grunted. "His blood. I couldn't stop." Jessie lifted his body up and stared at Nate with wild eyes.

"I didn't want to." The fear and anguish that had filled Jessie's voice were gone – replaced by something else. Kayla leaned in closer as Jessie continued.

"He deserved everything he got. I should have ripped him limb from limb after the vial things he did. I should have burned down the house with him inside. But no," Jessie's lips pulled back and a sinister grin flashed across his blood-stained face.

"Nate," Kayla stepped closer. The look in Jessie's eyes was vengeance. She had seen it before. A vision of Matt flashed in her mind's eye and she moved carefully around the furniture to Nate's side.

"Stop."

"What?" Nate glanced at Kayla. Jessie lunged at Nate with his mouth open wide. Kayla's arm flew out cracking against Jessie's face and sending him hurtling into the cushions of the couch. Alice screamed as Jessie rose up, ready to attack again.

"I said 'stop'." Kayla glared at Jessie using every bit of her mental strength to restrain Jessie from any further attacks. Jessie chopped and bit the air as he hissed.

"Alice, go upstairs. You don't need to see this." Kayla warned as she kept her eyes locked on Jessie.

"Nate, take Alice upstairs."

"Kayla, what is going on?"

"I think Jessie is possessed."

"What?" The shock in Nate's voice stabbed Kayla's heart. There wasn't time to explain, and she knew it. Jessie laughed hysterically as Nate rose to his feet and walked over to Alice.

"Come on, Kayla's got this."

"But?" Alice protested as Kayla sat down in front of the raving Jessie. His eyes bounced from Alice to Nate before coming back to Kayla. Kayla remained locked on him as she glared.

"You will tell me what happened."

"You know what happened," Jessie grunted as his voice cracked. From deep within his eyes, Kayla saw the struggle going on within Jessie. A fire burned within him and he was trying to regain control of himself.

"You will talk one way or another," Kayla warned and she lifted her hand up and clamped her fingers around Jessie's throat.

"I killed him. I did it for you." He hissed while Kayla's grip grew tighter.

"I would never ask for a life."

"I know," Jessie laughed. "That is why I did it. Because you never would, you are too weak to do what must be done."

"Who did you kill?" Kayla demanded as she applied more pressure around Jessie's neck causing her fingers to tingle from the strain.

Jessie pressed his lips together into a tight line refusing to answer. His head whipped around as Kayla struggled to hold him still.

"Who?!"

"Ha ha ha," Jessie's voice broke and a female voice spoke out of him.

Kayla let the laugh linger on the air for a brief moment as she studied Jessie. His eyes flickered as his body trembled. The sinister laughter filled the room. Kayla grunted and pulled her lips back.

"I've had enough out of you." Kayla pulled back her other hand and sent it flying. The crack of her knuckles against Jessie's face echoed throughout the house. The laughter stopped and Jessie went limp in Kayla's hand. Carefully, Kayla set Jessie down on the pillow and sighed. Her head throbbed just as much as her hand did. She glanced up towards the stairs to find Nate and Alice watching her.

"You can come down now," Kayla said as she stood up. Jessie rested peacefully on the couch and Alice rushed to his side.

"We need help," Kayla whispered to Nate.

"Okay, but whom?"

"I think Adam might be able to help. He knows a lot about the spirits and helped me prep before. Maybe he might know something to help us now."

"I'll go," Nate offered and he wrapped his arms around Kayla and pulled her in close. The warmth of his body soothed her and she buried her head in his chest.

Desire reared its head again. Kayla's hand drifted down Nate's body and cupped his cock in her hand.

"What are you doing?" Nate asked pulling Kayla away. Kayla shook her head, and glanced up at him. Her eyes drifted to her hand on him and she quickly pulled it away.

"I'm sorry. I don't know what's came over me. But I should go get Adam. Alice might need your help restraining Jessie if he wakes up."

"You would do a better job of restraining him than I would."

"No." Kayla shook her head. "I need the fresh air."

She leaned in closer to Nate and pressed her lips to his cheek. "I won't be gone long. Jessie should be out for a while. Stay here with Alice."

"Kayla," Nate's eyebrows pulled together and concern washed over his face. Kayla sighed as Nate tried to find the words. She gave him a brief smile and nodded.

"I know. I love you, too."

Kayla stole one more glance at Jessie before she turned. Nate pressed his lips together struggling to let her go.

"Hurry back though, okay?" Nate tried to smile, but his pain overwhelmed him. Kayla nodded as she walked out the front door. The patter of the rain hitting the roof filled Kayla's ears as she scanned the shadows.

"Is that all you can do?" Kayla thought, hoping that the spirits could hear her thoughts. She walked to the car and got in. The engine rumbled, and then Kayla gasped. A dark figure was hovering in front of the car. For a moment Kayla wondered what good it would do to run it over.

"I can do much more than that." Kayla's ears perked up as she heard the spirit. Her heart pounded in her chest and she threw the car into reverse and stepped on the gas.

"Maybe you should pick on someone who will fight back," Kayla countered as she spun the wheel around and raced down the street. She glanced into her rear-view mirror and saw the dark cloud following behind her. She knew she could never out run it, but she wouldn't give it an easy target either.

She turned the wheel and skidded around the corner. Adam's house was only three more blocks away. If she could get to him, she knew she would have a fighting chance. As she pushed the car through the red light, she glanced in the rear-view mirror. The darkness was gone and only the street lamps and houses filled the mirror. Kayla sighed and slowed the car.

A chill on the back of her neck sent her body into convulsions. She glanced over towards the passenger's seat. A dark figure sat calmly beside her with its hands folded, staring at the black river that was the road. Kayla gasped trying to remain calm. She had seen spirits before, but this one was far from pleasant. The vibe that flowed from it filled Kayla with a fear she hadn't felt in years. But she knew she couldn't let the fear hold her hostage. She had to stand her ground. Her eyes drifted from the road to her unwelcome passenger.

"What are you doing here?" Kayla demanded, hoping her fear didn't leak out in her words. The shadowy figured turned its attention to her and stared at her, its white eyes piercing her soul. Kayla jerked the wheel as she stepped on the brake. Her only hope was to get to Adam's as fast as her legs could carry her.

Kayla reached for the door handle as rain pelted the car. For a split second she dropped her gaze and the darkness shrouded her. Through the thunder and the rain, a single voice rose above the noise.

"Making things right."

Chapter 4

"Kayla? What are you doing here?" Adam stood in the open doorway staring at Kayla. She studied him as he stood before her with nothing but a towel wrapped tightly around his waist. She smiled and put her hands on his bare chest.

"I need to talk to you," she said batting her eyes. She screamed within her head, struggling to get control of herself. The darkness within her overpowered her will forcing her back even further into her subconscious.

"Adam, help!" Kayla screamed out, as she continued to smile at him. Adam glanced around her before stepping aside.

"Come in. I'll go and get dressed first and then we can talk." Kayla walked into the room and glanced around. Everything about the room was fuzzy. She tried to take control of her senses as she moved to the couch.

"You don't need to get dressed." She turned to face Adam, playing with the button of her pants.

"What are you doing?" Adam stepped back from her, and he grabbed her wrists stopping her from going any further.

"Taking what I want and right now. I want you."

Kayla lunged at Adam pressing her lips to his. Adam didn't move. He kept her hands at bay as her lips parted his. Kayla slipped her tongue into Adam's mouth and rolled her tongue around his.

"Maybe we should take a moment," Adam huffed suppressing his desire as he stared at Kayla.

"I don't have a moment."

"Is Nate here?"

Kayla smiled as she shook her head. "No. But you are."

"Where is Nate? I thought you two were a thing."

"We were a thing. But after tonight I don't think he will be much of a problem anymore."

"Is that why you wanted to talk?" Adam dropped Kayla's hands and stepped back from her. Kayla moved forward keeping the space between them tight. Her eyes fluttered to the towel around his waist as the smile grew across her face.

"I would rather not talk. Not unless our fingers do the talking." Kayla reached out for Adam. In one swoop, she tugged the towel off his waist. Her eyes widened as she stared down at his member. Without hesitation, Kayla dropped to her knees and took his cock into her mouth.

"Maybe we should think about this," Adam began to protest as Kayla devoured him. The warmth of Kayla's mouth drowned out all hesitation. He threw his head back as his fingers curled into her hair.

"I think I am going to be sick," Kayla groaned as she tried to stop herself. Never had she thought of Adam in this way, despite how stunning he was. Ever since she met Nate, no one else matter. Kayla tried to find a way to stop herself, but the darkness was relentless. It knew precisely what turned Kayla on and how to press her buttons.

"Do you want me to stop?" Kayla asked glancing up at Adam.

His head bobbed up and down as he said, "No."

"Tell me, what is it you want?" Kayla stroked the length of his shaft as her hand drifted down to her pants.

Adam's eyes were on her as her fingers inched their way under the fabric.

She opened her mouth wider and relaxed her throat, driving his cock further down. Every inch of Adam's cock filled her mouth as her head bobbed faster and faster. Adam groaned with pleasure as Kayla played. With one hand she cupped his balls and rolled them in her fingers.

Adam's fingers tightened in her hair forcing her to remain latched to his cock. Soon, it was Adam's tugging and pulling that instructed Kayla's mouth. She hummed as she swallowed his cock down her throat. The vibrations of her song unraveled Adam's passion. He pulled her head back causing Kayla's back to arch in order to look up at him.

"I hope you know what you are getting yourself into," Adam said with a smile.

"I hope you know what you are getting into," Kayla mimicked as Adam released his grip on her hair. She scrambled to pull her pants off as Adam dropped to his knees. He jerked open Kayla's legs forcing her to expose herself to him. Kayla couldn't deny herself as her pussy begged for attention. The need for something long and hard pounding her filled her every thought.

"Give it to me," Kayla demanded as Adam grabbed his cock and pushed it into Kayla's eagerly awaiting body.

"Yes," she hissed as he filled her. "No!" Kayla screamed in her head fighting back the darkness as it took control of her.

"You are so tight," Adam panted as Kayla's body wrapped around his penis. Even Kayla couldn't deny how thick he felt. He rammed her harder, stretching her out more than Nate ever had. Each time the crown of his cock slipped from her, Kayla gasped. Her body yearned for more and she knew that even Nate could never fill the hole that was growing inside her.

She wrapped her legs around Adam's body forcing him to stay in her longer. She moved as he moved, both joined at the hip and fighting for domination. Kayla racked her nails down Adam's strong back as they slid about the wooden floor.

"My turn," Kayla panted as she squeezed her legs around Adam's waist, pulled herself up and twisted. Before Adam could stop her, he landed hard on his back. Kayla spun around him carefully lifting one leg up as she moved. She faced the front door as she rocked her body against Adam.

Every muscle in her body was on fire as she drove herself further down on his rod. Adam grunted taking all that he could of her.

"Yes," Kayla screamed over the sound of her phone as it chirped. "Fill me. I want to drain your balls and make you cry out for me to stop. Then I want to do it again."

"Damn woman," Adam cooed as Kayla's lowered her body. Her hand slipped between their legs. The moment she touched their bodily fluids, she covered Adam's balls with it. She smiled to feel how hard everything was. From the tip of Adam's cock to his throbbing shaft, down to his ball sack, everything was strong and hard.

"That's it," Kayla cried out rocking faster as her fingers slipped over her clit. "Right there."

"You are going to make me come," Adam said gasping for air.

"That's the idea." Kayla giggled as she moved faster. Their bodies slammed against each other as the passion consumed her.

"I'm..." Kayla didn't need for Adam to finish the rest of his sentence. His hot come shot into her body filling her and quenching the fire that burned inside of her. Every fiber of her being unhinged as she threw her head back.

"Holy hell," Adam panted.

"What?" Kayla asked glancing over her shoulder with a smile on her face.

"Is it always like that with you?"

"Like what?" Kayla wondered as she slipped Adam out of her and crashed to the floor trying to regain her breathing.

"So intense."

"I don't know. You will have to ask Nate about that."

"Crap, Nate." Adam sat up and rested on his elbows. His eyes widened as he stared at Kayla.

"What happened to Nate?"

"Nothing as far I know," Kayla smiled as she tried to get up. Her legs wobbled under her weight and her weak muscles throbbed. She moved carefully over to Adam and snatched her panted from beside him.

"Kayla," Adam's reasoning came back to him and he glanced around his home. He shook his head as remorse filled his eyes. "Where is Nate now?"

"Right here."

Kayla shifted her eyes to the front door to find Nate standing with tears in his eyes. In the deepest part of her being, Kayla pushed through the darkness to find Nate staring at her with disbelief. The sinister laugh filled her head as a piece of her shattered like glass on concrete.

Kayla knew the look. It was the same one Jessie had given Alice, the night Kayla and Nate had invited her into bed with them.

"Jessie," Kayla blinked as the fog cleared and allowed her to see perfectly clearly. She shook her head as if waking from a bad dream and glanced around the room.

"Oh no," Kayla's voice was barely audible as she pushed one leg into her pants and then the other.

"Mind telling me what is going on?" Nate glanced at Kayla then Adam. Adam scurried to grab his towel and wrapped it quickly around his waist to cover himself.

"She wanted me," Adam said in his defense.

"Did she now?" Nate's stare stabbed Kayla more than any blades could have. "Well, don't let me stop you two from continuing. After all, who cares about Jessie right now?"

"Nate please let me explain," Kayla reached out for Nate. He stepped back dodging her advance as he shook his head.

"I don't need an explanation. You take what you want when you want. That's your thing right?" Nate's words cut her, and she pulled back.

"Did you even bring up what has happened to Jessie?" Nate demanded as Kayla glanced at Adam.

Slowly Kayla remembered why she came to Adam in the first place. She dropped her head and shook it. Shame filled her as she tried to remember what happened.

"Or was coming here to fuck him the only reason why you left?"

"Nate, it wasn't like that. I didn't know."

"What that you would get caught? That I would show up here? Or is that what you wanted? You know Kayla, if you didn't want to be in a serious relationship with me there are other ways to tell a guy. But this," Nate's hand flew around the room as Adam stepped back and sat on the edge of the couch.

"Nate please, let me explain."

Nate pressed his lips into a tight line and shook his head. "Forget it. I will figure out what's wrong with my brother. Don't worry your pretty little head."

Before Kayla could say another word, Nate turned and stormed out. Kayla wanted to go after him, but knew he needed time. She needed time to figure what was going on.

"You know, you don't have to listen to him. You are the rightful alpha and with that come specific needs that can't be tamed."

"Such as?" Kayla retorted, glancing over at Adam. Her heart shattered into a million pieces as Nate climbed into Alice's car and sped away.

"Well, for one thing, this. Sex with multiple people. A true alpha has issues staying faithful. I think that might be why Nate didn't want that for you in the first place. He was scared of losing you to the temptations."

Kayla shook her head. Her initial reasons for coming to Adam began to filter through her pain. She snapped her head up.

"We need to talk."

"Yeah, that's what you said. But I need a few minutes to regroup. You're one wild animal in the sack you know that?"

"No; not sex, talk. Something is going on and the spirits are not happy."

Adam's brow scrunched as he studied Kayla. She nodded and sucked in a deep breath.

"You're right, we should talk." Adam rose from the couch. His eyes flickered to the towel around his waist.

"Maybe you should get dressed first," Kayla said turning her eyes away from him. "And wear something loose. I don't think I can handle your sexiness right now. Not until we figure out what is going on."

Chapter 5

Kayla sipped the hot tea. Her eyes lingered on the grooves in the wood as she tried to piece together the last few hours. But every time she tried to focus on the darkness, her mind grew fuzzy.

"What is the last thing you do remember?" Adam asked taking the furthest seat from Kayla. She glanced up at him for a brief second before dropping her eyes back to the wooden table.

"Going to Alice's place. She came over to Nate's, crying her eyes out. She said something had happened to Jessie. So, we went over to her place only to find Jessie out of his mind. He was covered in blood."

"Whose blood? It could have been an animal he attacked, while he was in wolf form."

"True, but what if it was a person? He was after all mumbling and shaking like it was his first kill." Kayla dared to look at Adam. Despite his loose rugged shirt and jeans, Kayla still found him sexy as ever. She turned her head away and sipped on her tea.

"But he was saying they deserved it. So wouldn't that imply he killed someone?"

Adam nodded and stood up. He paced the length of the table keeping as much distance between himself and Kayla as possible in his small dining room. Every so often however, Kayla caught a whiff of his musky scent and the passion sparked again. She pressed her lips together and held her breath. There was no way she would be caught off guard again. Not with Nate already hurting from want she had done.

"So, you told Nate that maybe I could help. Why?"

"Because you know a little about the spirit world. I thought maybe you could tell us something. Has anything like this happened before? Has a newly appointed alpha gone crazy or lost their mind briefly? Because that is what it seems to have happened to Jessie."

"Honestly, I don't know. Sure, there are stories of alpha's going mad because of the pressure, but I don't think there are any stories of them going to the extreme of killing someone. I know that if I were an alpha, I wouldn't be able to handle the pressure of it all. Maybe Jessie just snapped, but I wouldn't know for sure."

"Well what about what happened to me?" Kayla fought back the tears as she glanced at Adam.

"What happened to you?"

"I came here to talk to you about this stuff. I didn't expect to attack you. And the thing is – it wasn't me. There was something in the car with me. It attacked and the next thing I know, Nate is here and we were..." Kayla's words drifted away like smoke. They both knew what they had done and she couldn't bring herself to think of it again.

"So, that wasn't you I played with?"

Kayla pressed her lips together and shook her head. Refusing to look at Adam she pulled her mug to her lips and sipped the hot liquid.

"Okay, that's a little discomforting."

"A little? That stunt just cost me my relationship with Nate."

"Maybe the spirits don't want you to be with him and decided to take matters into their own hands, so to speak."

A light bulb went off in Kayla's head. She stood from her chair and gasped. "What did you just say?"

Adam stopped pacing and turned to her, "They wanted to take matters into their own hands?"

"I remember," Kayla's heart drummed in her chest as the sinister voice played back in her mind. "It said it was fixing things. Making things right." Kayla stared at Adam as her memory flooded back.

"Is it possible that when we crossed over, we brought something back with us? I mean Jessie was supposed to stay there. Those were the rules, and I broke them by bringing him back. What if I left a door open for something else to return as well?" Kayla's eyes widened at the same time Adam's did. They stared at each other for what seemed like an eternity.

"You should probably talk to Eric. He will know more about this than I do. He was the last alpha after all."

"But he wasn't the true alpha. He was only holding the position."

"True, but he was the leader. Maybe he had heard something similar. But I will see what I can find and call you."

Kayla nodded and pushed the mug away from the edge of the table. "I am headed over to Eric's. I will let you know if I find something too."

Kayla smiled briefly at Adam as she walked to the door. A part of her wanted to hug him, but she couldn't trust herself not to attack him again. After all, if there was something still inside her, she wanted it out and fast.

With Nate's car keys still in her pocket, she walked over to the car. She sucked in a deep breath and pulled open the door. Nate's scent filled her nostrils as she climbed in. Tears swelled in her eyes as she started the car.

"I will make it up to you, Nate, I promise," she mumbled and she started the car. Glancing over her shoulder she studied the long, dark road. The rain had stopped some time ago leaving the black asphalt slick. In the darkness, it looked like a placid river flowing through the town.

When she was certain nothing was with her in the car, she pulled out of Adam's driveway and headed towards Eric's. Kayla knew it was a long shot going to Eric. She also knew Eric was still on the fence about her. But if Jessie was involved, he would want to know about it.

She drove carefully through town. At each dark alley she slowed and peeked into the shadows, half expecting to see something. But as she made her way to the other side of town and to Eric's place, the only thought that came up was Nate. The look in his eyes pained her more than she could bear and now she was going to have to face his father.

Kayla pulled over to the curb and sat in the car staring up at the house. A dim light filtered through the curtains of the window. "It's now or never," she huffed.

She unbuckled her belt and got out of the car. With her hands in her pockets, she walked up to the front door. Her hand trembled as she reached for the doorbell. A small chime filled the quiet house and she took a step back, waiting for him to answer.

Chapter 6

After the bell got no answer, Kayla rapped her knuckles against the door and waited some more. When there was no sign of movement she peeked around the corner to glance into the house. The lights remained on and she wondered if someone was upstairs. Moving to the front yard, she tilted her head to stare up into the darkened window.

"Maybe," Kayla wondered as she made her way around to the back. The contents of her stomach dropped like a ship going over waves in a turmoil ocean. Her eyes grew wide with fear as she came to the back door. The screen door was split open as if a battering ram had pushed through the thin material. The closer she got, the more the waves in her stomach tossed about. Her footsteps thundered as she walked up the three stairs and pulled the door open.

"Oh shit," she gasped covering her mouth with her hands. Blood dripped from the kitchen sink and was splattered on the floor below. She jerked her head away as the smell filled her nose and burned her nostrils. Quickly, she took her cellphone out of her pocket and dialed as the fresh night air swirled around her. On the other end, the line rang continuously.

"Pick up," she whispered, tapping her foot. When there was no answer, she hit the end button and tried a different number. The phone rang twice before Alice's voice came on.

"Nate doesn't want to talk to you right now," Alice hissed. Clearly news of what she had done was spreading fast. But Kayla didn't have time to argue with Alice over her mistakes.

"Where's Nate?"

"He's here with Jessie, but I really don't think he wants to talk."

"He doesn't have to. But he does need to get over to Eric's." Kayla's eyes shifted to the house. Her heart sank as she tried to find the words to tell her.

"Why are you at Eric's?" Alice asked and her voice dropped. Kayla wondered if Jessie and Nate were standing next to her, listening in on the conversation.

"It's not something I can say over the phone. Just get here and fast."

Kayla hung up the phone, as dread stabbed her chest. She moved slowly back into the house. Sucking in a deep breath, she held it for as long as she could and stepped further inside. Eric was resting on the floor with his head in a pool of his own blood. His dinner sat untouched on the table.

Kayla glanced around the room looking for more signs, but her lungs burned from lack of oxygen. She bolted for the door. The moment the cool air caressed her face she sucked in a deep breath and knelt over. Headlights flashed past her as Alice's car pulled up next to Nate's in the driveway.

A new pain ripped through her as she saw Nate climbing out of the backseat. Jessie wobbled as he pulled himself out of the passenger's side. Alice stared at her with accusing eyes as she cut the engine and joined the boys on the lawn.

"This better be good," Nate snapped.

"That is not a good choice of words," Kayla sighed.

"Why?" Jessie's eyes flickered to the house as he shook his head. Tremors rocked his body as he stared at the house.

"Jessie?" Alice wrapped her arm around him as she tried to keep him together.

"No." Jessie's voice was barely audible as the tremors brought him to his knees.

"I'm sorry," Kayla said fighting the urge to go to him. She knew that she was no longer welcome in their circle. She was once again the outcast and them coming together as a unit reminded her of their bond. Kayla swallowed the lump in her throat as she stepped to the side and lifted her arm up to the house.

"You may want to brace yourselves. The smell is overwhelming."

Nate glared at Kayla as he walked past her. The coldness in his eyes stung, but she knew she deserved so much worse. Alice and Jessie moved carefully towards the house. Kayla glanced at Jessie. His eyes were filled with horror as he tried to remember. Kayla wondered if she had had that same expression when Nate had found her with Adam.

"No!" Nate screamed, catching Alice off guard. Alice dropped her hold on Jessie and raced to the door. Nate dropped to his knees and tears poured out of him.

Alice followed and cupped her hands over her mouth as she turned towards Jessie.

"What?" Jessie asked. But Kayla knew the answer was already breaking through his haze. His memories were returning. Judging by the way the light filled his eyes Kayla knew the flashes that were coming back to him weren't good. Jessie's face turned a whiter shade and Kayla winced.

"Oh God, no. I..." Jessie dropped to the ground, shook his head and curled up into a fetal position. His face was white and fearful. Kayla moved over to him and dropped down by his side. Her arms were around his shoulders and she kept her gaze on him. He trembled under her, as he wept uncontrollably.

"I know," Kayla said in hushed tones. "You didn't do this though. You can't blame yourself."

"But I did. I remember." Jessie wailed as Kayla squeezed him closer to her.

"Something is going on with us. I think we may have brought something back from the other side." Jessie turned his attention to Kayla and she dropped her head as she confessed.

"During the challenge, one of us was meant to stay there. But I couldn't leave you in that place. It wasn't right," Kayla continued as she licked her dry lips.

"But by bringing you back, I may have brought back something or someone else also."

Kayla hadn't realized Alice and Nate were by her side as she spilled her secret. She shook her head as Naku filled her mind. The Indian woman with such a vengeance for her children had stolen the very warmth from her blood. Chills raced down Kayla's back as she thought of the ghost.

"Are you saying he's possessed?" Nate asked, his hands balled up into tight fists at his side.

"It's possible." Kayla glanced back at Jessie. "Are you having issues remembering parts of the night? Or is everything fuzzy? Like you're not in control?"

Jessie nodded and Kayla's suspicions were confirmed. "I felt the same way three hours ago. It's like you are a puppet and someone else is pulling the strings."

"But why would Jessie kill Eric? They're family." Alice stole a glance at Jessie. A smile was growing on Jessie's face and a wicked laugh ripped through his trembling body.

"He deserved to be killed. I should have burned the house down with him inside. I should have ripped him limb from limb. But I wanted to see the light fade from his eyes as he bled out." Jessie said through the sinister laughter.

Kayla rose from the ground and stepped back. The color in Jessie's face had returned – a brighter shade of red as he continued to laugh. Nate's pressed his lips together into a tight line and flung his hand back before crashing it into Jessie's jaw. Jessie flew into the air and landed on his back. Kayla gasped as Nate shifted into his wolf form. Alice ran to Kayla's side.

"Stop him before he kills Jessie," Alice pleaded as Kayla tried to figure out who had taken over Jessie.

"Stop this right now. It's not going to help if you two are at each other's throats. We need to find a way of getting that thing out of Jessie."

"Good luck," Jessie hissed as he shed his human form. Nate growled and lunged for Jessie. Roars bounced off the houses, and the neighbor peeked through the window before quickly shutting the curtains. Kayla growled as she watched Nate and Jessie attacking each other.

"Jessie, Nate, stop right now." Kayla ordered to no avail. She stepped back as the two clawed and bit each other. Nate pulled back and with an open mouth lunged for Jessie's throat. Jessie sidestepped him and nipped Nate's flank as they brawled.

"I can't get through to them," Kayla gasped as she and Alice stood watching them roll into the tree line behind Eric's house.

"The only way to stop this is to figure out who came back with us and put them back."

"What about Jessie and Nate?" Alice asked as Kayla turned her attention to the house.

"I don't think they will kill each other. The sooner we figure out who's inside Jessie the better chance we'll have of stopping the bloodshed. Come on. Help me see if there isn't something in the house that will help us figure this out."

Kayla moved towards the house as the roars and growls echoed through the darkness. She sucked in a clean breath of air and pushed herself into the house.

Chapter 7

Kayla held her breath as she moved further into the house. She tried not to stare at the remains of Eric as she moved around him.

"What is that?" Alice's voice surprised her. She spun around and exhaled losing the air she had trapped in her lungs. Her mouth dropped open as she saw the writing on the wall.

"I did it," was written on the wall leading to the stairs. Kayla glanced at Alice before turning her attention up to the dark second floor.

"Maybe we'll find something up there," Kayla said, walking to the steps. She began climbing them with Alice on her heels, as they made their way to the upper floor.

"I don't understand why this happened to Eric," Alice said, turning her head turned from side to side. "I mean, he was Jessie's dad. Eric never did the spirit journey, so why was he targeted?"

"Naku once said Eric was an interloper and an imposter. Maybe she is behind this."

"So, just make contact with her and make her stop."

"That's just it, ever since I stepped down from the alpha position, I've sort of lost the connection. She doesn't answer me."

"Maybe she is ignoring you and doing her own thing. Maybe she is the reason this is happening. She is trying to take out the family that is standing in the way of you becoming alpha."

Kayla turned and stared at Alice. "I never thought of that."

As the thought danced around Kayla's mind, the two of them continued to search the bedrooms upstairs. Kayla nodded to Alice as they came to two doors.

"Take that room. I'll do this one. Let me know if you find anything,"

Alice's eyes widened. "You want to split up? Haven't you watched any horror movies? This is always what happens and the characters end up dead."

"Alice, we aren't going to die." Kayla reached into the open door and flipped the switch. Light flooded the room and she smiled.

"And for the record, I have watched horror flicks. And usually the lights never work."

Alice glanced into the room and let out a soft laugh. "You're right, it's just..."

"I know. But the sooner we can get answers, the sooner we can stop this. Now, go."

Kayla didn't wait for Alice to respond. She opened the second door and went in. Kayla scanned the room. Nothing about it seemed off. She walked to the closet and reached for the door knob but then she heard Alice in the other room.

"Kayla! I think you need to see this."

Kayla joined Alice in the second bedroom, but hesitated as she noticed Alice staring into the closet.

"What did you find?" Kayla moved to Alice's side and glanced into the closet. Three shelves lined the back wall and images filled them. She stumbled back when she saw the images. Flashes of her brief time with Matt filled her mind.

"A trophy room," Kayla gasped. With a trembling hand she reached out to the second shelf where she plucked a picture off the shelf. Her heart drummed in her chest and her stomach twisted.

"Who is that?" Alice asked glancing over Kayla's shoulder to look at the family in the photo.

"Those are my parents," Kayla said staring at the young girl with a smile on her face. She swallowed hard forcing the words out of her mouth.

"Matt had the same picture."

"Then maybe it's Matt who came back?" Alice stated as Kayla dropped the picture causing the glass to shatter at her feet. The very thought of Matt returning, frightened Kayla more than anything else in the world. She knew he was a violent criminal who stop at nothing to get what he wanted. And the motives were all there.

Kayla concentrated and the mystery began taking shape in her mind. Everything was connected; from Kayla's family to Eric's death and even Naku. Each piece shifted as the picture of Kayla's future came into view. Matt would want to take out Eric because he submitted to Kayla after the spirit journey. Matt would want to take out her too, or at least destroy the one thing she cared about the most.

Before Alice could say another word, Kayla turned and stared at her. "Call the police. Get them over here to clean this mess up. And try to find Jessie and Nate."

"Where are you going?" Alice asked as Kayla sprinted out of the room, down the stairs and out the back door.

Kayla's head swirled and thoughts filled her mind. She couldn't take it anymore. Before she hit the tree line, she shifted into her wolf form. The only thing that soothed her was her nails digging into the soft dirt at her feet, as she sprinted to the forest. A long howl echoed around her as the sun broke through the trees.

"Nate?" she thought as she felt the pain of the howl. She shook her head forcing herself not to care as she went deeper into the woods. She didn't know where she was going, but she knew she needed time to sort things out. There was only one place she could go to find peace, and that is precisely where she didn't want to go.

Chapter 8

"I thought I might find you here."

Kayla turned her head and lifted her hand up to shield her eyes. The sun broke through the trees as the rumble of tires against the asphalt filled her ears. The crisp clean scent of wet wood filled her nose and a gentle breeze picked up the loose strands of her hair. A familiar scent of musk and lavender was on the breeze. Kayla forced herself to smile as Adam walked up behind her.

"How did you know?"

"Well, I am a damned good tracker. I caught your scent earlier this morning."

Kayla's cheeks turned a shade of red, and she glanced down to the white cross. She sucked in a deep breath as the leaves crunched under Adam's footsteps.

"So why are you here?"

"Actually, I think I've found a way for you to fix what's going on with Jessie." Adam said and he pulled out a small vial from his jacket. Kayla's glanced at the brown liquid before shivering.

"You want me to go back to the spirit world?"

"It's the only way for you find out who exactly came back with you and to close the door."

"I know who came back: Matt."

"The one who killed your parents?"

"Who else could it be? He killed them," Kayla nodded to the cross as her words broke. "I killed him. He is pissed that the status has passed to me."

"I don't think it's him."

Kayla crossed her arms and glared at Adam. With one eyebrow raised she stared without saying a word.

"Look, he wanted you dead and out of the picture. But, he wouldn't take out the people he was working with before. I think Naku is behind this. That woman has always wanted her daughter to take control. She is going after the other family that is forcing your hand to step up."

Kayla's mouth dropped as Adam connected the dots. The missing piece she hadn't seen before was so obvious it pained her.

"I can't believe I missed it. I mean ever since I turned it down, she hasn't spoken to me. I thought the whole spirit thing was behind me. But..."

"But when you pulled Jessie out of the spirit realm, she tagged along too. She saw you pull him out and knew that only a true alpha had the power to do it. She played you. This was her intention the whole time. She needed you to go. She needed the contest to take place to force you into her world so that she could be a part of yours."

"I really have screwed everything here haven't I? I shouldn't have come here. I should have stayed in the crappy truck stop and never ventured into the mountains that night." Kayla dropped her head and tears poured out. She wiped away the wetness and turned to Adam.

"Look, I know you think that everything is your fault, but it's not. What happened between us…" Adam cleared his throat as he stepped closer and put the vial into Kayla's hand. "…it wasn't you. It was Naku, she knew that Nate would come looking for you. She knew what would happen if Nate found you with someone else. That is why she did it. She wanted you to be separated from everyone, to claim your title."

"Adam," Kayla sobbed as she glanced at the vial in her hand. "I can't go up against her. I can't face Nate or anyone."

"You have to. You are the only one who can. If you don't, Nate's life will be in danger. Don't you see? Naku won't stop. She will use Jessie to kill Nate and then she'll kill Jessie. Or maybe she is hoping that Nate will take out Jessie and then transfer into him and take him out. Her end goal is simple. Do whatever is necessary for you to become the alpha; even if that means killing everyone in town. You have to stop her."

"Then what? I kill Jessie and lose Nate forever because I took out his brother? All these different paths only lead to more death."

"Not if you pull her back into the spirit world. You have to find a way or Eric will be next."

"Eric is the one Jessie killed," Kayla confessed and she glanced up at Adam through her blurred vision. She wiped away the tears as Adam stumbled back in shock.

"Then she is already starting to take them out one-by-one. Kayla, please. If you don't do this now, you risk killing Nate. If Naku is in Jessie, she won't be holding back and no one has seen them for a couple of days."

"Which means they might already be dead." Kayla gasped as she clutched the vial. Her heart pounded in her head. Despite the pain in her chest from her heart shattering, she knew Nate deserved a better ending. She popped the lid off the vial and pressed it to her lips.

"I will be right here when you wake up."

"How do I know you aren't Naku?"

"You're just going to have to trust me." Adam winked as Kayla lowered herself to the ground and drank the contents of the vial.

She sucked in a deep yawn and sleep washed over her like a warm blanket. "Here we go again."

Kayla's closed her eyes and lay back with her head beside her parent's cross. As she settled, the wetness of the grass irritated her, seeping into her clothes. She wondered how long she was going to have to wait for the concoction to kick in. Each second that passed only irritated her further. The last thing she wanted was to be wet and cold.

"Adam, I don't think this is working," Kayla grumbled and sat up, scanning the area for Adam. No matter which way she turned, he was nowhere to be seen. Kayla rose to her feet and wiped the dirt from her backside.

"Adam?"

"No," a husky voice answered. Kayla whipped her head around to find Eric standing before her consumed by blue flames.

"So it did work," Kayla huffed as she stepped closer to Eric.

"Yes, and I know why you are here," the old man said, stepping away from Kayla so as to keep his distance from her.

"Then tell me how to stop this," Kayla sneered but Eric only shook his head.

"I didn't mean for it to go this far. I didn't know it would end like this."

"Eric, I don't have time to mess around. Where is Naku?"

"Jessie," the moment Eric said his name, Jessie appeared before her. Kayla clasped her hands around her mouth as she saw the red flames swirling about him. Kayla's heart sank as she reached for Jessie.

"No, you can't pull me out this time. She made sure of it," Jessie said and he glanced over at Eric. The red and blue flames danced around each other but never mingled. Kayla nodded and remorse filled her.

"I didn't want this to happen either," she said, sighing deeply. "So how do I fix it?"

"First, I must apologize for my part," Eric moaned as the surrounding flames grew and licked his skin.

"Your part? In what?" Kayla glared at Eric and questions filled her mind. But she knew she didn't have time to ask them all. She wasn't here to save Eric, she was here to find out how to close the door she had opened and to make things right.

Eric cleared his throat trying to expel the smoke from his lungs. Kayla realized speaking was getting harder and harder for the old man. Eric lifted up his hand and forced the words out of his dry throat, "The death of your parents."

Kayla's eyes widened and she stared at Eric in disbelief. He lifted his finger up and pointed behind Kayla, trying to control a coughing fit. She turned around as the trees faded away, and they were standing in a small living room. Kayla stumbled back as she saw her mom and dad beside Matt and Eric.

"I won't follow that girl," Matt sneered, while his face turned a darker shade of red. Kayla noticed he was beyond mad when he threw his hands up in the air in disgust. "She cannot lead us."

"Not right now, she is just a babe, but in time she will," Kayla's mother spoke in soft tones coddling the small child in her arms.

"The spirits have wanted this for a long time. Even you can't deny that, Matt. Now, they will finally find the peace they have been waiting for. We may even be able to lift this curse."

"What if we don't want it lifted?" Eric snapped. "The speed, and power, this is not a curse but a blessing. We live outside of nature, and with nature. Why would anyone want to give this up?"

"Because we weren't meant to stay like this. The spirits had hoped that Tomoku would yield but instead he took her life." Kayla's father stepped over to and stared down into the child's wide eyes.

"It is done," Kayla's father said, straightening his shoulders. He turned his attention to Matt and Eric. "It has been written."

Kayla reached out to touch her parents, but as her fingers brushed over their faces, they vanished like smoke. She glanced over her shoulder to Eric, who dropped his head.

"Are you sure they are coming?" Eric asked and darkness filled the area around Kayla, Eric, and Jessie. Kayla's eyes widened as the long black road stretched out before her.

"Patience," Matt said as he stared down the long road. "I can smell them. They won't be much longer."

"Maybe there is another way?" Eric asked, but Matt just jogged to the side of the road.

"Do you want this to end? Do you want to obey a girl?" Eric shrugged. "Well I don't. Now do your part and leave the rest to me."

Kayla didn't need to see anything else. She knew what was about to happen as the headlights of her parents' vehicle came into view.

"No!" Kayla cried out as Eric remained in the middle of the road. The car swerved and Kayla covered her eyes waiting for the scene to unfold. She shook her head, listening to the exchange between her mother and Matt.

"I deserved what I got," Eric said finally. Kayla uncovered her face and stared at him. Anger, hatred, pain, loss, every emotion she had ever had filled her. But, as the flames licked at Eric, she realized there was no torment or justice she could wish on him that wasn't already being inflicted on him.

"Jessie is innocent. I know that you pulled him back before because you are kind and would be a great leader. But the only way for him to go back is if you vanquish the one who is now in control of him."

"I don't even know where to start looking," Kayla said, staring at Jessie.

"You will find us by the river. But you must hurry, Nate is in bad shape."

"Go please and stop her before I lose both my children," Eric pleaded as Kayla glanced around the area searching for a way out.

"You helped to kill my parents. You tried to stop me from taking my place more than once. Why should I stop Naku from doing to your family what you did to mine?" Kayla spat as she stepped away from Eric trying to control herself from shifting.

"Because you love Nate," Jessie answered. "Your love for him is stronger than the pull of the sun. He is calling for you."

Nate's face flashed into Kayla's mind. She knew she would do anything to mend things with Nate. She sighed letting the frustration seep out of her fingers.

"What I do next I do for Nate," Kayla said as a bridge appeared in the forest. "But, you must tell Nate that I never meant to hurt him."

"I think he understands that it wasn't your fault, by now," Jessie said as Kayla ran past him. She stopped shy of entering the bridge.

"Tell him," Kayla ordered. Jessie nodded as she stepped onto the platform. White light filled her eyes and she shot up from the ground.

"That didn't take long," Adam said extending his hand to help her up.

"Longer than I wanted."

"So what now?" Adam scanned the area as the sun's rays shot through the trees.

"Now I need to find Jessie and Nate before something really bad happens to one or both of them."

"I'll come with you."

"Are you sure you want to come?"

"Look, I know Nate doesn't like me right now. But Jessie and I have been friends for a really long time. I can't just sit here and wait. I have to do something to help."

Chapter 9

"How well can you track?" Kayla asked as she pulled her phone out from her pocket. She knew she needed a backup if Nate didn't answer her call. She dialed Nate and waited. Adam smiled.

"I found you didn't I?" he answered her question.

"Yes, but can you find Nate or Jessie?"

"Yeah, that's easy." Adam pointed towards the forest. "They would be by the river."

"How do you know that?"

"That's where they always go when they scrap."

"Come on then, we need to find them and fast."

Before Adam could protest or ask any further questions, Kayla let the tremors take over her body. The heat flowed through her and she shed her human form. With her big eyes, she stared at Adam waiting. He shrugged and let the wolf out.

The instant Adam was in his wolf form, Kayla sprinted towards the river. The dirt scrapped between her paws and she pushed herself to go as fast as she could. She filled her mind with different scenarios of how she might find Nate in order to prepare herself for the worse. The last image she saw was of Nate lying dead on the river bank. The image upset her, so she sprinted even faster. Her heart broke as she pushed through the shrubs.

"He's not dead," Kayla told herself again and again. "Nate can handle himself. He will be fine."

After the forest cleared and she arrived at the river's banks, Kayla calmed herself. The fire within her went out as she saw a body on the other side of the calmly flowing stream.

"No," she gasped and she shifted back to her human form. Adam skidded to a stop. His muzzle went up into the air and he whipped his head to the side. Kayla didn't have to know what he was saying, the look in his eyes gave her all the information she needed.

"Go," she said as her heart dropped to her stomach. Adam took off sprinting down the bank and disappeared over the hill. Kayla steadied herself as she wrapped her head around the idea that she may not have gotten here in time.

Slowly she made her way through the chilly water until she came to the body. With a trembling hand, she touched it and sighed.

"Nate," Kayla gasped and she dropped to his side, shaking him. Nate groaned and Kayla lifted his head onto her lap.

"Thank God you are still alive. Where is Jessie?"

Nate's eyes fluttered open and he focused on Kayla's worried face. A small smile played at the corner of his lips and then he forced himself to get up. The happy reunion turned sour as Nate wobbled under his weight.

"I didn't expect to see you here," Nate winced and reached for his side.

"Nate, I know you don't like me right now, but please, you have to tell me, where is your brother?"

"Why? Do you want to fuck him too?"

"Your brother is possessed."

"Likely story. I suppose you are going to tell me you were too, when you were with Adam?" Nate's eyes narrowed and Kayla dropped her head.

"It doesn't matter. You are going to believe whatever you want. But whether you believe me or not doesn't matter." Kayla lifted her head and stared at Nate. She rose slowly and faced him. The glare in his eyes rattled her nerves, and she realized there was no going back to where they were before. She nibbled on her lower lip trying to find the right words.

"Look, I need to find Jessie. Something is wrong with him."

"Don't I know it. He didn't pull his punches." Nate lifted his arm up showing a chunk of flesh that was red and angry from Jessie's bite. Kayla covered her mouth with her hand, watching it heal.

"Put aside your anger towards me and tell me where you last saw Jessie."

"I left him about five miles down the river." Nate nodded towards the direction of where Adam had gone. Kayla's ears perked up as a howl echoed through the trees. She started to shift, but then paused. She stole a moment to stare at Nate one last time.

"I know I hurt you. Believe me, I didn't want to. I am sorry for everything."

"Sorry won't fix things Kayla."

"I know. But at least I said it," she pressed her lips together as her heart shattered. She nodded once and turned her back on Nate as she shifted. Then she raced towards the direction of the howl, sweeping up the pieces of her heart and filing them away in a tiny box at the back of her mind.

"I will always love you Nate," Kayla thought as she ran. A second howl filtered through the trees and she knew she was getting closer. Kayla ran through the shrubs and low-hanging branches, coming up short at the sight of Jessie and Adam circling one another.

The hair on Adam's neck rose with each pass. Jessie's growls exposed his teeth as he nipped the air in front of Adam. Kayla knew Adam was no match for Jessie and with Naku inside of the wolf, he would be killed.

"Stop this, right now," Kayla demanded as she dropped her wolf form and stood before them. Adam glanced at her and moved back from Jessie. Jessie snapped and bit at the air between him and Adam, and the hairs on his back spiked. Kayla's eyes drifted over to Adam, ensuring he was safe before she took a step closer.

She raised her hands in the air to show no signs of aggression. Jessie's head whipped back and forth trying to figure out whom to attack first.

"Jessie, I don't want to hurt you. But I will if you attack me," Kayla said moving in closer to force Jessie to focus more on her, rather than Adam. Adam stepped back once again. Kayla crossed in front of him giving him the escape route he needed. The moment Adam was out of range of Jessie's teeth, he shifted into his human form and stumbled back some more.

"Jessie?" Adam's voice wavered as he realized his friend was no longer in control of the wolf's body.

"Adam, that's not Jessie and you know it," Kayla stated keeping her hands up. She circled around the beast trying to corner it between the river and herself. The last thing she wanted was to see Adam hurt.

The large wolf snapped at the air as Kayla drew closer. She didn't flinch as the wolf growled and barked. A smile grew on Kayla's face as she watched the animal backing away.

"Naku, I know you are in there. Give up. You have nowhere left to go."

Jessie snapped his jaw shut and growled.

Kayla spoke again. "I will hunt you to the ends of the earth if I have to. Now let Jessie go."

Chapter 10

Kayla's eyes widened as Jessie's body trembled and shook violently. It was clear that the spirit did not want to give up its wolf form, but somehow it was being forced to do so. Kayla stole a glance at Adam while Jessie's wolf's coat dropped to the ground, revealing the man underneath. With a spark in his eyes Jessie laughed. Adam glanced at Kayla, waiting for her to give the word for him to attack. Kayla shook her head ever so lightly while keeping her eyes locked on Jessie.

"I was wondering when you would figure it out," Jessie's voice cracked as he spoke. The undertones of a female voice filtered through.

"Let him go," Kayla demanded holding her ground.

"Why? The linage needs to die before you can realize your true potential."

"It will never happen. I will never be alpha of this tribe. That was never my destiny. And neither was this for Jessie. You stole his life just like your husband stole yours. Don't you see, you are only making things worse?"

"But it is your destiny!"

"No," Kayla shook her head. "It isn't destiny. It's what you want. Your goals and admiration for the position have driven you mad. I saw what happened. I know firsthand what happened so long ago. You just wanted your firstborn to be blessed. Instead, it was your second born that got the glory and you couldn't just be happy with what you had. You took matters into your own hands and now here we are. You've made Jessie a murderer."

"What's done is done. There is no way for me to return." Naku hissed through Jessie, as Kayla dropped her hands.

"There is a way, you just won't accept it. I see that now. No matter what I do, you will find a way to come back and haunt me. You will never let this go."

"Wait what?" Adam's jaw dropped as he stared at Kayla with wild eyes. "She has to go back. She can't stay here. What about Jessie?"

"Jessie is trapped in the spirit world because you stole his life." Kayla glared at Naku. "You stole his life, his family, and his destiny. Jessie doesn't deserve the fate you have forced on him. And you will allow him to return."

"No, he took what was yours," the spirit sneered, stepping back from Kayla.

"No, he didn't. I didn't even know my place until I came back here by accident. If I hadn't made that journey through the mountain pass, I wouldn't have been a part of any of this. Eric would still be alive, and Jessie would have taken his place as the leader. Instead, I came and threw everything out of balance. If you want to be mad at someone, be mad at me. Take my life and give Jessie back his."

"Kayla what are you doing?" Adam reached out for her trying to get between her and Jessie. Kayla glanced at Adam with a stern glare and shook her head.

"Don't you see, you are doing to Jessie what Tokomu did to you? It is a vicious cycle that I am going to end right now."

Kayla rushed Jessie with her arms stretched out. Before he could turn and run, she dug her fingers into his skin holding him in place. Jessie thrashed trying to free himself from her grip, but to no avail. Kayla was locked on to him like an eagle to its prey. She lifted her head up to the sky allowing herself to release everything she had built up for so long.

Every emotion flowed out her. Kayla thought of her parents and how she had lost them so young. She thought of Eric and what he had said to her. She allowed her mind to linger on Matt and pushed through the anger of what he had done to her. Finally, her thoughts rested on Jessie as she stared into his eyes. Kayla pressed her lips into a tight line as she prayed for the first time in her life.

"What are you doing?" Jessie growled as the wind kicked up around them. Kayla's hair whipped about her forcing her to close her eyes. But her mind was made up. She filled her lungs full of air as she prayed and broke down the walls she had built up over the years.

"No." Jessie screamed, and Kayla's eyes opened. High in the sky, she saw a great white wolf hovering above her. Jessie's thrashed in Kayla's grip trying to get free. Kayla held Jessie down as the wind pulled Naku out of Jessie's body and returned him to the spirit world.

"Kayla what are you doing?" Adam's voice was muffled by the gusts of wind. She smiled at him before pulling Jessie closer to her.

"Relax," she said to Jessie as she leaned closer and pressed her lips to his.

The wind settled and Kayla pulled away from Jessie. He blinked the darkness from his eyes and stared at Kayla with wonder. Her smile grew as Jessie pulled in a deep breath.

"Kayla?" Adam hesitated to come any closer. She turned her head to him and laughed.

"It's over," Jessie said bewildered. Kayla shook her head and pulled Jessie into her. She wrapped her arms around him, burying her face into his neck.

"I am so sorry," Kayla said before pulling away. "But she will never hurt you again. I have made certain of that at least."

"I can't thank you enough." Jessie squeezed Kayla into one of his bear hugs cutting off the flow of air to her lungs.

"Well, you can start by letting me go," Kayla huffed, gasping for air. Jessie laughed and released his grip around her. "Then maybe you can patch things up with Nate."

"Oh God." Jessie's eyes widened as he glanced around the area searching for his brother. "I almost killed him. Where is he? Is he okay? I couldn't stop."

"He is fine," Kayla reassured. "You will find him down the way." She nodded her head down the river.

"He will never forgive me."

"Sure he will. It will just take time. After all, you're family." Jessie squeezed Kayla and kissed her on the cheek.

"You should probably go and find him. Set things right, you know?"

"Aren't you coming with me?" Jessie asked waiting for Kayla to move. She shook her head with a small smile. "You should probably go alone. After all, you two have a lot to talk about."

"Kayla I..." Jessie began and Kayla patted his shoulder.

"I know. Now go find Nate and make up. I am sure he will be relieved to have his old brother back."

Jessie smiled and took off back down the river leaving Adam and Kayla alone. Adam stepped closer to Kayla and laughed.

"In all my years, I never saw anything like that."

"Well, hopefully, you will never have to see it again."

"So what do you say we head back and get a drink? I don't know about you, but I could use something strong."

"You go and have one for me."

Adam had already turned to leave but he paused. Kayla turned her head towards the open space of the forest beyond the river and sighed. The leaves rustled as the wind called to her.

"You aren't coming back are you?" Adam said with concern written across his face. Kayla shook her head before turning to face him.

"Adam, you saw what happened. Do you really think I could just go back? Besides, no one wants me there anymore. Nate was the only reason why I stayed to begin with. Now that we are done, there is nothing left for me to go back to."

"But you defeated her. You won. Surely you and Nate will make up and things will go back to the way they were, you know before all this."

"I didn't win anything."

"This is about Nate isn't it? You think he won't forgive you."

"I know he won't. I also doubt you will be his favorite person for a while. What we did can't be undone. But hey," Kayla forced a smile to filter through her pain. "At least everything will go back to the way it was for you. Maybe one day, for him as well."

"Before you came here," Adam said realizing Kayla was trying to say goodbye.

Kayla nodded and pressed her lips into a tight line forcing the tears to remain locked away. "Do me a favor?"

"Anything," Adam said as Kayla sucked in a deep breath.

"Make sure Nate learns the truth about everything and tell him I will always love him."

"Count on it. But..."

Before Adam could say another word, Kayla let the fire ignite within her. Her body shimmered and twitched as she shifted into her wolf form. She stole one last glimpse at

Adam and whimpered before taking off into the deepest part of the forest.

Chapter 11

The chirping of birds high in the boughs of the trees soothed Kayla as she soaked in a hidden spring deep in the forest. The warm water eased her strained muscles. She closed her eyes allowing the water to wash away her sorrow. She couldn't remember the last time she had had a bath.

Being in her wolf form for so long was a new experience, but she understood why others chose to remain that way. All her doubts and human emotions were stifled by the wolf. She didn't feel the stab of losing Nate. But here, in the empty space of the forest, all those emotions flooded her once again.

"You know, you don't have to live like this."

Kayla stared down into the clear water. Her wet blonde strands, draped around her neck like seaweed, faded to black as Naku stared back up at her. Kayla splashed the water trying to rid herself of the image of Naku.

"Come on, you know you don't want to live like this. You enjoy the human world too much. Denying yourself is only going to make you unhappier."

"Naku, I made a choice and I am living with the consequences. We both knew you wouldn't go back to the spirit realm without a fight. This was the only arrangement that I could think of at the time. So enjoy this moment while it lasts. The moment I am cleaned up, we are shifting back and moving on."

"But you sacrificed everything."

"Please," Kayla sighed. "Don't remind me of the things I lost and I won't remind you."

"Kayla, I never meant for it to go this far. All I wanted was for you to take your place as the rightful leader."

"Naku, you can stop now. I know what you wanted. You have been living in my head for months now. I know everything you do."

Kayla tried to focus on the sounds of the birds in the trees and the summer breeze kissing her face. But her heart was breaking just the same. She knew the only place she wanted to be was with Nate and she also knew how impossible that was at the moment.

"We can always go back," Naku said as Kayla dunked her head under the water trying to drown out

Naku's voice. But the stillness of the water only amplified the voice in her head. Kayla held her breath for as long as possible before returning to the surface.

"Kayla, please, let's go back. We can find another tribe, or even live in a city somewhere around people who don't know about us."

"No. We can't. You made sure of that and I don't want you being tempted to jump into bodies and cause any more havoc."

"I won't do that. Now, I understand why you never wanted to be the alpha. I was wrong to force you into that position. It was wrong of me to take Eric's life, but you have to understand why I did it."

"Oh I understand why. I just can't see how you can justify your actions. I would never have done anything like that to anyone. The only reason I killed Matt was because he attacked me. It was in self-defense."

"I know," Naku sighed as she stared up at Kayla through the water's reflection. "I know you love your freedom as well. I took that from you. Even now, as you keep me in your body, I am stealing that from you. I know how even being with Nate was a strain for you, but you did it. You found a home, and I took that from you."

"Naku, stop. I don't want to hear you anymore right now okay? You got what you wanted. You didn't go back to the spirit world, you are here. Now please, let me finish my bath in peace." Kayla's irritation grew. She pulled herself from the water and shook herself. The water from her hair sprayed about her like diamonds. When the last diamond fell, she walked over to a fallen tree and sat down.

The snapping of branches behind her startled her. Kayla sprang to her feet ready for a fight. She took a deep breath, waiting for the attack. The scrunching sound of leaves being trodden on drew closer. Kayla's body trembled and she started to shift into her wolf form. Suddenly, though, she stood up straight. The musky scent of woods, mingled with lavender and lemons, swirled around. Her eyes scanned the trees as a dark figure emerged from them.

"Kayla?" Her heart fluttered as she heard her name.

"Nate?" There he was stepping out of the shadows and into the light. His hair was a bit longer, and he smelled more of the forest than of the lavender fields that grew wild on the mountain near his village. For a moment Kayla wondered if she had lost her mind. She stumbled back nearly falling into the spring behind her.

"What are you doing here?" Kayla stepped back fearful of what Naku would do to him if he wasn't a vision. But the longer he stayed in one place, the more certain she became that he wasn't a figment of her imagination.

"I have been tracking you for months. I thought I caught up with you last week, but I missed you by a few hours. Then the storm came through and I lost your trail. But now I've found you," Nate sighed with relief and looked at Kayla. The spark in his eyes was something she was not expecting. She dared to step closer.

"I wanted to talk," he said moving in with a smile on his worn-out face.

"You shouldn't be here. It isn't safe."

"Jessie told me what happened. He explained everything. And when I saw Adam at the diner, he passed your message along."

"Did he now?"

"He told me everything," Nate moved closer taking his time approaching Kayla. She could see he was timid and as unsure as she was about the situation.

"So is it true? Is Naku inside you?"

Kayla sucked in a deep breath. She didn't want to lie to Nate, but she didn't want to tell him the truth. Kayla glanced at him then let her eyes drop to the ground.

"I see," Nate nodded and he stopped his advance. Kayla glanced up at him. More pieces of her heart fell away as she tried to fight back the tears.

"Look, you should go. I'm fine, really. But you don't belong here. I'm not stable."

"Do you remember what I told you before?"

Kayla's eyebrows rose as she tried to figure out what he was talking about. They had many conversations on many occasions, but the precise moment he wanted eluded her.

"Nate, we had our time. It's over. You have to move on."

"I told you that I wanted all of you. The wolf and the girl."

A small trickle of water spilled from the corner of her eye as the memory played back in her mind.

"I still mean that. I want you." Nate took a step closer. Kayla's heart pounded harder in her chest with each step Nate took. She raised her hand up to stop him. His fingers curled around her wrist. Without warning, Nate pulled Kayla to him. The heat from his body scorched Kayla. It felt like forever since she had had another person pressed up against her. Nate smiled as he cupped his hand around her face and pressed his lips to hers.

"I'm sorry I didn't believe you," Nate whispered as he pulled away. Kayla stared up into his eyes. She shook her head and pushed him away from her.

"I'm sorry I couldn't control it. I am sorry about your father. I wish ..."

"Don't. None of this is your fault. Things from the past collided with the present and what happened, happened. How we handle this is what makes us strong." Nate dropped his head and pressed his forehead to Kayla's as he held her.

"I promised to be by your side always, and at the first moment of distress, I turned my back on you. I am so sorry for that."

"Nate I love you. I will always love you."

"That's all I needed to hear."

"Then you should go now."

"But why?"

"I can't be with you right now. Not with Naku still inside of me. What if she decides to take over and be with someone else? What if she falls in love with another, then what? Having her in me makes things so complicated." Tears spilled out of Kayla as she clung to Nate. In her heart of hearts she couldn't bear the idea of him leaving her, but she knew it was the right thing to do, to keep him safe.

"We will deal with it when we cross that bridge."

"You shouldn't have to deal with anything."

"Kayla, I love you more than anything else in this world. If you won't return to mine," Nate stepped away from her and stripped off his shirt. Kayla watched as he worked on the buckle of his pants. The heavy fabric dropped to the forest floor leaving Nate just as exposed to the elements as she was.

"Then I will join yours," he continued.

"I won't share you with her. I can't. I won't." Kayla wiped the tears from her cheeks shaking her head. She stepped back widening the gap between Nate and herself.

"You don't have to. Adam found something in his books about a way to draw her out of you. She can go in peace."

"I don't understand."

"Adam found a past alpha who took frequent trips to the other side to get knowledge for the tribe. Often he would come back with them attached to him like Naku is attached to you. Adam knows of a way to fix this, but..."

"But I have to go back with you."

"Please Kayla," Nate reached out for her. Kayla stared at his hands while hope filled her.

"Kayla, go back with him. I am ready to leave this place," Naku said as Kayla remained uncertain.

"If I go back, you have to promise me that I will never have to go through something like this again."

"Jessie will never ask you to."

Kayla hesitated before stretching out her trembling hand. She stared up at Nate with hope. The pieces of her broken heart mended the instant Nate curled his arms around her and kissed her.

"Come on, let's go home."

Epilogue

"That's it?" Kayla's eyes were locked on the tiny vial in Adam's fingers. She sucked in a deep breath before reaching for it.

"That's it. Pretty nifty, huh?"

"What does it do?" Kayla asked taking the vial from Adam.

"Well, essentially it will rid you of the spirit allowing them to be set free."

"How does it taste?"

"Seriously? You are more concerned with the flavor than what it does?" Nate shook his head as he laughed at Kayla.

"You try tasting the other stuff and then tell me if you aren't a bit wary about this stuff. These old potions taste like crap."

"Just do it and get it over with," Adam grumbled as Kayla popped the top and put the vial to her lips. She pinched her nose with her other hand before draining the liquid into her open mouth.

"There, now swallow," Nate chuckled watching Kayla's face turn a shade of green. Kayla swallowed hard forcing the stuff down her throat.

Her toes began to tingle and soon her leg went numb. Her eyes widened as she looked at Adam. "I can't feel my legs," she panicked.

"Relax, that is supposed to happen."

"Really? Are you sure about that? How often have you taken this potion?"

"Kayla, trust me," Adam smirked walking back to the couch and plopping down.

"Adam, so help me if anything happens to her."

"Nate, Kayla, will you two please relax? The herbs are pulling out Naku from her toes to her head. Will Kayla go completely numb? Probably. Will she get the feeling back? Most likely."

"Most likely? Maybe? Adam." Before Kayla could finish her sentence, the herbs worked their way up her body. Every fiber tingled and sizzled as Naku laughed inside Kayla's head. She wanted to ask what was so funny, but her head was jumbled and confused. For a moment she didn't know which way was up or down.

"You know, if you ever wanted to take the lead," Adam smiled at Nate. "Now would be the time to do it."

"What?" Nate flashed daggers at Adam as he threw his hands up in the air.

"I'm just saying. Those herbs are strong. I doubt Kayla will be functional for a while. You could easily take advantage of her right now."

"You might do that, I would never."

"Really? Never?" Adam's lips pulled up at the corner as he teased Nate.

Nate turned his attention back to Kayla. She was sitting on the edge of the chair letting the herbs ground her. Peace filled her the instant Naku left her body. She blinked at Nate and smiled.

"Wow."

Every inch of her felt new. It was as if her entire body had been scrubbed from the inside out. Every nerve and fiber tingled as they came back to life. Kayla jumped up from her seat and crushed her lips against Nate's. The sensation was electric. Kayla wanted more. She lifted her leg and curled it around Nate's body as Adam laughed on the couch.

"Kayla?" Nate mumbled through her lips.

"Take me now."

"If I was you, I would do as she says," Adam chuckled as Nate scooped Kayla up into his arms.

"I can see myself out," Adam said rising from the couch. "I am sure you two would like your privacy."

The sound of the screen door slamming against the wooden frame thrilled Kayla. She nibbled on Nate's neck as she reached for his shirt and ripped it over his head.

"You want the lead?" Kayla asked. Nate smiled and shook his head.

"I just want you."

The End.